THE HELIOS SYNDROME

Typesetting: Ryan Vance

THE HELIOS SYNDROME

VIVIAN SHAW

"Lemme guess," says Chief Investigator Dooley of the NTSB, peering over my shoulder at the crystal ball. The image inside it is distorted because of the curvature of the crystal, but it's recognizably the cockpit of a Boeing 737. Or the remains of one. "It's the langoliers."

"It's not the langoliers. I'll let you in on a little secret, Dooley, I'm not actually supposed to be telling you this, but it's *never the fucking langoliers.*"

"You disappoint me, Stacy," he says. "I want my expectations managed with more integrity. Okay, so what the hell *is* it?"

"Well, that bit there's supposed to be the circuit breaker panel, except for the fact that it's completely detached from the wall. And over here we got what used to be the airspeed indicator—"

Inside the crystal, a moray eel undulates across the picture from right to left. It must be four feet long. "Dang," says Dooley. "Big sucker. My point *is*, what transpired to bring about the current situation vis-a-vis the location of the cockpit and presumably the rest of the bird on the floor of the fucking ocean, including the hitherto elusive black boxes? We kinda need to get an answer on that part."

"You don't say," I tell him, bone-dry, and straighten up so he has to quit looking over my shoulder. "That's not why you assholes pay me, or anything. Listen, Dools, I kinda need to concentrate here, so if you don't mind I'd appreciate a little peace and quiet?"

"My sincere apologies, *Contingency Communications Specialist Stacy*," he says, enunciating. "Do let the rest of us know when you've consulted the goddamn oracles and got us a probable conclusion, okay?"

I flip him a salute, and keep my face straight until the door shuts behind him—and then I don't really care if the security cameras pick up my *fuck you, jerkwad* grin. Wayne Dooley and I have been working together on and off for three years now, and the fact that he is an asshole of the purest ray serene kinda makes it okay for me to be an asshole *right back*.

Let me back up a little. I'm Devin Stacy. Yeah, I know "Devin" is supposed to be a girl's name, and yeah, I've heard literally every single Stacy's Mom joke the living and the dead can come up with. What the Board actually pays me for is billed under the job title of *contingency communications specialist* because somehow *freelance necromancer* just doesn't have that bureaucratic ring to it. I get brought in when the rest of the National Transportation Safety Board—scene investigators, lab scientists, analysts, the whole boiling of 'em—can't figure out why a plane went down. All of their tests are coming up clear, or the flight data recorder and cockpit voice recorder show absolutely nothing of use, or they simply don't have the physical evidence to determine a plausible explanation for the crash: that's when I get the phone call. *We got one, Stacy,* and these days it seems like it's always Doolarino on the other end of the line, instead of any of the other investigators I've worked with. Which chaps his ass about as much as it does mine, but what can you do when the Board's biggest dickhead seems to be the one catching all the unsolvable cases?

The current problem I'm looking at in my storied crystal ball is *what made a FedEx 737 decide to go swimming somewhere in the South Pacific with only a couple tiny bits washed ashore to show for it like in that Tom Hanks movie,* and they're lucky as hell they even *have* those tiny bits, because without them I wouldn't be able to do a damn thing. I don't have the range or sensitivity on my astral projection needed to scour thousands of miles of super-deep water—but with a piece of the plane to use as an anchor, I picked up where the rest of it was in about twenty minutes. What I'm trying to do now is locate the black boxes, which stopped pinging their radio locator beacons a while ago. The plane went down six weeks back and they couldn't find it within the limited lifetime of the beacons, even with towed sonar *and* remotely operated robot subs tracing expensive search patterns across the ocean floor. That is, in a nutshell, why they called in yours truly: I cost less per hour than the robot subs and I'm way more entertaining.

The cockpit is the first thing I'd managed to get, holding the shred of purple-and-orange metal in my left hand and cupping the crystal in my right. The cockpit's always the first to come, because it's the soul and center of the plane, its brain and heart: it's the heaviest weight on reality. But I think I can find Dooley his recorders, if I put enough effort into it. I know I'm gonna wind up with a migraine in return for that effort—this shit is not easy, not by any means—but hey. Three people died in this crash, and there's enough of this goddamn plane species still flying that we really need to know what brought *this* one down.

(At least it's not a passenger flight. At least that. The accident airplane's flight plan had a cruising altitude of 36,000 feet, and falling from that height makes water as unyielding as solid rock. If this plane had been full of people, we'd have a hell of a lot of empty caskets getting buried. Three's bad enough; three hundred would have been a whole lot worse.)

I change my grip on the shard of metal and *focus*, pushing my conscious awareness through my gaze into the crystal and out the other side, to the place I'm seeing—and I'm prepared for it, but the sudden shock of cold as I'm surrounded by the psychic equivalent of seawater is still enough to make me gasp. In a way I'm *there*, two miles down, in the unrelieved darkness of the deep ocean; if I lean on this hard enough I'll come back to find myself drenched in *actual* seawater. In my jacket pocket are a couple of battery-powered radio-transmitter beacons; if I do find the black boxes I'm supposed to push those through to mark their location so the searchers can pick them up. It's a balance, keeping enough of myself this side of the crystal to maintain control, shoving enough of me through to get a good image of what I'm observing.

The debris field is … well, it feels *wide*, and the pieces of wreckage aren't all of equal size. Some of the cockpit had been intact, if damaged, but most of the bits I'm looking at now are barely the size of a sheet of paper. Because this wasn't a passenger flight I don't have the additional challenge of a whole chorus of three hundred screaming ghosts frozen in the middle of a terrible death; it's eerily silent, for a wreck. The crew, all three of them, aren't really here anymore. Once they hit the water at pulverizing speed, there's little left but fragments, and three weeks at the bottom of the ocean turns even substantial human bits into something unrecognizable, even to someone like me. I can sense a faint queasy anguish and terror in the water, but nothing I can ask useful questions of.

I reach out further, feeling for the knots and snarls of time and space that are the cockpit voice recorder and flight data recorder. This is the part of the job that's most exhausting ... and the part that often winds up with me lying down in a dark room for hours until the sparklies go away.

The boxes stand out to me, to the kind of sight I'm using; it's not exactly like seeing a light in the darkness, or feeling a source of heat in the cold, but that's the closest I can come to describing it. I could actually—*probably*—pull the recorders themselves back through with me if I tried very hard, but the paperwork involved in that kind of stunt makes even the most jaded Board agent go funny colors and I'm not sure I wouldn't have a stroke, so all I do is plant the radio locator beacon device on each. That *hurts*, moving physical objects from plane to plane is like lifting weights with your brain, and I'm falling backward out of the trance. I open my eyes then immediately regret this, because hello there, migraine—and instead of Chief Investigator Wayne Dooley standing there snapping his fingers at me it is a man without a face, just churned scarlet meat strewn with little white chips that had been teeth, blood almost but not quite obscuring the captain's stripes on his shoulderboards.

I barely manage not to say, *Oh fuck, not again*, out loud.

My primary job is talking to the dead on behalf of paying customers, whether they're private citizens or the federal government, thus the freelance necromancer bit. I'm good at my job, even if I am mostly self-taught, and I've been doing this since I was maybe seventeen. I know how to do it, is my point here. There's a whole ritual you're supposed to do in order to summon the dead person and bring them through to this plane of existence, it's got gross ingredients and blood and chanting and shit just like you might expect from necromancy. But this time it's happening without the usual business of the circle, chalk, or quartz points: this time, Captain Warner's found his way through on his own. Again.

*

I'd give the migraine three out of five stars, this time. Didn't puke, but wanted to. It was over in a few hours; I was able to drive myself home before the worst of the blowback hit. After that kind of spellwork I always feel fragile, like a guy made out of glass blown too thin, which is why I am lying on my Ikea couch and half-watching Great British Bake Off ... and trying with a total lack of success not to think about Captain Fucking Warner and whatever he might want from me.

He's a ghost, of course. There's sorta-kinda a difference between straight-up ghosts and spirits who are Beyond The Veil (happily or unhappily, but them's the breaks) that I summon with my handy circle. Ghosts aren't done with *this* plane of existence—that old bit about them having unfinished business is totally true. They just hang around until exorcised by ceremony or the good fortune of a remedial psychopomp. Or until whatever it is they're stuck on finally gets resolved.

But Warner feels different, though. Warner feels more substantial than the ordinary ghosts I've dealt with. Sometimes you make a stronger connection, an immediate rapport, with one of the departed. As soon as Warner came through my circle, he'd manifested strongly enough to actually grasp my hand amid the smoking, reeking wreckage of his plane, and just like that I was in his cockpit when it had still been in one piece, grey utilitarian plastic. He was insistent enough to draw *me* through, rather than me being in control of the situation, and that in itself was freaky: what he showed me then was freaki*er*, to the point where I don't even want to think about it, let alone remember in enormous detail.

Dooley hadn't been able to see him. Dooley couldn't see a ghost if it put a bedsheet over its head and gibbered; the dude is without the slightest psychic susceptibility. Maybe that's why he's such a cynical but effective investigator. Working for someone intelligent, even if they're totally obnoxious, is better than working for someone who sucks at their job.

Having to debrief Dooley while Captain Warner stood there and dripped spectral blood in a meaningful sort of way *right beside him* is not going to be one of my most treasured memories of this employment opportunity. Dime-sized drops of blood splattered the floor, and as I was telling him I'd planted the beacons on both recorders another drop splashed on the polished toe of one of Dooley's expensive wingtips, and for a few seconds there I really did think I was going to hurl.

This is four or five times now that I've seen Warner, since the Mount Storm crash that killed him nearly a year ago. That was a bad one even by my standards, and the actual cause was not something I could code on a Board report; I had to fudge it, and say lightning fried the plane's avionics beyond recovery. It wasn't lightning, of course. Not *regular* lightning.

(I know Dooley doesn't believe my report. I also know that for reasons of his own he has never publicly contradicted my conclusions, presumably because a closed case is better for his stats than an open one. No clue what *he* thinks about Mount Storm, of course, and no way to know, unless it's somewhere in his endless stacks of yellow legal-pad notes.)

Mary Berry is doing that thing where she purses her lips just slightly and the baker is fucking crushed, because they know the flavor isn't *quite quite*—fuck, I can't concentrate, the image of Warner's cockpit keeps coming back: perfectly ordinary 737, nothing wrong at all on the instruments, green across the board, forward-looking weather radar black and clear, and out of the front windows a vast supercell is suddenly boiling, bruise-dark and killing-wide. It's the kind of weather you don't fly into unless you want to dance a tango with the worst turbulence of your life: rudder-snapping, airframe-tearing air, out of nowhere. And in the dream-vision Captain Warner has seen it, but his first officer has not, and what Warner wanted to tell me, *show* me, was what waited for the plane inside that cloud.

I was with them, in this dead man's memory; I was there while Captain Warner stared mesmerized into the boiling blackness of that thundercloud, and as—too late, much too late— he wrenched the plane into a steep left bank trying to avoid it, but he knew and I knew and the first officer now knew that it was much too late because we were now past the fringe and in it—immediately violent turbulence struck, shaking us like rats in a trap, like dice in a cup, like anything you want to fucking name—behind us the passengers were screaming, and I could hear luggage crashing down as the overhead bins shook open—the windows were blank grey-black except for the white-violet flares of lightning all around us, it was as if the plane had been held in the grip of some terrible hand drawing us into the very heart of the storm and *still the radar screens were black and clear—*

The next part I don't want to think about. The next part I'm not even really sure about; only that something underneath us, five miles down, looked up and saw us. Saw *me*. Saw me very well, and smiled.

I'm not supposed to mix the migraine meds with alcohol but I think with visceral clarity *fuck that all to hell*. There's good scotch and mediocre scotch, and maybe the good kind can blunt the memory barrage more quickly. Seeing Warner brings it back. He appears out of nowhere, wanting something I can't understand—and because I can't understand it I can't give him whatever the hell is on his non-existent mind and send him off into the great black yonder to find what awaits. I wouldn't mind so much if he wasn't so fucking *gross*. Or if he didn't set off a good old-fashioned cascade of Devin Stacy's Traumatic Memories every time he manifests.

I've tried asking him. Summoned him for real, with the crystal and the chalk and the herbs and the right phase of the moon, and all he does is show up like he always does, faceless and dripping blood and gray matter, looking at me with the eyes he hasn't got until I let him go again. Most uncommunicative dead guy I ever ran into, and of course it turns out he's the one who ends up haunting me.

And now that I think about it, it's been happening pretty much every time I do any serious, significant magic shit for work: I guess just garden-variety chatting to the dead doesn't get his attention, but recently, every time I go astral-projecting, it's been Warner who's there afterward. Waiting for me like some hideous fucking groupie after the show.

It is for once an actual pleasure when my phone buzzes and DOOLEY appears on the screen: talking to Dools can be grounding out of sheer annoyance. Chief Investigator Wayne Dooley looks pretty much like a well-groomed version of the Mayhem guy on those Allstate commercials and has this smug, gleeful, shit-eating grin he is pleased to employ when he's asking someone to do something they really don't feel like doing. Ask me how I know.

I settle back on the couch with two fingers of something much too expensive to drink the way I'm drinking it. "Why, Investigator Dooley," I say. "What strange concatenation of circumstance is behind this, you never call me unless it's four in the morning and you want me to do work."

"Black boxes," Dooley says, all business. "The beacons you planted did the job, they found 'em right away. Looks like we're gonna get them to the surface in a few hours local time, then another twenty-four until they're shipped to DC and our analysis can begin."

"We know this to be true," I say. "So what?"

"So I need you to stay on call until we get those recorders. When we play that data back I want you to listen to it with your special ears, okay?"

"Oh my god," I say. "Special ears. What am I, a Keebler employee?"

"You know what I mean. Just be there, okay?"

"...Fine," I tell him. I got nothing on for the next couple of days, and it might be better to be working than fucking around on the internet and wondering if I'm cursed for all eternity to be followed around by a dead airline pilot with the communication skills of a brick wall and, if so, what the hell can I do about it?

*

The NTSB labs are less tidy than they appear on the Mayday show. The lights are ordinary overhead fluorescents; there is less soul-searching conversation between researchers, and definitely less of the pregnant silence broken by "By Jove, I've Got It" moments of inspiration. Also, the chairs are super uncomfortable.

The FedEx plane's black boxes—the battered flight data recorder and cockpit voice recorder I'd encountered recently at the bottom of the ocean—are orange, like every other plane's black boxes: they yell in giant letters FLIGHT RECORDER DO NOT OPEN.

In here we open.

Inside, depending on the age of the dead plane, is a tape recorder or a solid-state drive that may or may not hold useful information: what was said, and what the plane was doing. This time we got semi-lucky, according to Dooley's goons. He's got three of them at the moment, all baby investigators specializing in some individual system on the plane. They appear to have been brainwashed into developing some weird kind of hero-worship for their boss, judging by their collective expression, and they do not know what to do with me: I don't fit into the preexisting hierarchy of the team, and I don't have even a *single* advanced degree.

"Everything's totally normal until an hour before the end of the recording," says a goon, or a goonette: super on-trend crystal-clear frames and a clear desire to further her career by being noticed for something other than just being the only chick in the room. "There's just normal cockpit conversation, back and forth, until right about here."

"Roll it," says Dooley, grey eyes narrowed in a steely expression you just *know* he's practiced in front of a mirror. The tech goon pushes her button, and all of us lean forward just a little, listening. I close my eyes and listen *harder*, trying to pick up anything the technology might have missed.

The familiar hiss and crackle of cheap microphone pickup fills the lab. Small enclosed space, not a lot of echo. Two voices, both male.

"—gotta try to get my schedule fixed," one says. "Can't do this for three weeks in a row, it's screwing with everything else. I wanna get back on the Newark to LA run."

"Hah," says the other. "Good luck with *that*, they schedule guys like a damn lottery, last week I was in fucking Narita."

"Good bars there?" A third voice. The flight engineer. I haven't heard the cabin door open or close, so he must have been there all along.

"Wouldn't know. Never got a chance to do anything other than crash and get right back to the airport." A pause, then "—whoa, little bumpy out here."

"Sure is." There's rattling in the background, loose objects being tossed around, and a grunt from one of them. "—Damn. Belts on, guys."

A series of rustles and clicks. "On. You wanna see if this smoothes out or—whoa!" Thumps in the background: things falling. Doesn't sound like it's getting better.

"Fuckin' clear-air turbulence," the third voice says, disgusted. "Someone's gonna puke. Might be me."

"Let me see if we can just kind of get around this," says one of the first voices. "My airplane."

"Your airplane. You want me to get clearance to a different altitude?"

A pause, and then another series of clatters and grunts: evidently the guys up there had been shaken around pretty bad. "—if this shit doesn't stop, yeah—" and a moment later the sound of objects bouncing around begins to ease off.

"Man, that was bad for a minute." The voice sounds shaken.

"Your turn to file the PIREP," says the first voice. "And yeah, if that starts up again, get on to ATC for clearance. We got some breakable shit back there."

"Just make it so I don't spill my coffee any *more*," says the third, and there's a little laughter. After that, all three of them shut up.

We don't know what's happening; clearly the initial crisis is over, they're back to steady level flight. One of them is presumably working on the PIREP—more acronyms, I know; aviation is nuts for them. The *pilot report* informs air-traffic control of the turbulence, but nothing has been transmitted yet. I still don't hear anything in the background other than the hum of the engines.

"So what now?" says one of Dooley's less intuitive goons, and is elbowed silent.

A minute or two later one of the crew seems to take a very deep breath. It's hard to make out on the scratchy recording.

"Steve, do you feel a little different?"

"No, what's wrong?"

"Kinda strange all of a sudden."

"You want me to take it while you go get some water or something?"

"I dunno, it's—fuck, I feel strange, yeah, take it, your airplane."

A pause. More deep breathing. Still nothing behind them but that hum.

"—yeah," says the other man, "okay, I do too actually, it's like—"

They begin to talk over each other in little snatches of words that are hard as hell to make out. A cold finger touches the base of my spine: I know this one. I know what happens next. I know how *fast* this shit snowballs. I also can feel their distress, very faint, a kind of synesthetic echo from the voice itself. It's like being slowly submerged in cold water.

"—maybe the air in here is—"

"—something wrong with the air packs—"

It's getting worse. From here we start losing the edges of coherence. I can picture it much more clearly than I want to.

"—shit, something's wrong, Patel, get in touch with the ground, we got a problem here—"

"—roger I can't—the mike—can you reach— what—"

"—no the mike —here—fuck—can't do it— what—"

"—should—don—"

"—don—masks—checklist—"

The words are beginning to slur, rising in pitch as their fear and distress increases, the emotional echo harder and harder to think through. I know exactly what's happening, and I don't want to hear it happen, and I have to anyway, it's why I'm part of this, listening with my *special ears*. In fact I'm there, inside their terror, locked in the moment with them.

"—can't get it free—thing's stuck, fuck—"

"—here let me help wait—no—can't—still have—"

"—don't—what—"

"—I can't—" It's getting more and more incoherent, snatches of words. I can make out another couple of what might be expletives;

all I can feel now is terror and confusion and a growing kind of numbness, as if I'm freezing slowly from the ground up. We're listening to the CAM-1 and CAM-2 channels, cockpit area microphones that pick up whatever is going on in there, and that in itself is a problem because of what I *don't* hear in the background.

There's no cabin-altitude warning horns. No master caution. No bells and whistles at all. Just terror, growing numb.

(Very clearly, in my mind: Warner's plane, flying straight into a killing storm, its weather-radar screens still black and clear.)

"And then it just isn't verbal, and then there's nothing at all," says the goon, abruptly, and turns off the playback. "The rest of it is nothing but dead air, forty minutes of it before the recording ends. There *are* a couple slight differences shortly before the end, and we think that's the engines cutting out from fuel starvation, but other than that it's just the background noise. There's no engine flameout warning horn, no stick shaker once they start to slow down, no ground proximity warning system going *whoop whoop pull up* or *too low terrain, too low terrain* over and over as they get closer to the water, there's no master caution or any of the other alarms you'd expect at all, it's just—dead silent."

God, these guys had no idea what was happening to them. At all. At least it was quick:

of the ways you can die in a plane, this one knocks you unconscious in less than a minute at this altitude. And now I know what it *feels* like, hooray for me.

"Decompression," says Dooley, a second before I say "Hypoxia."

The goons turn to look at me. I shrug. "Somehow their—"

"—cabin lost pressure slowly enough they didn't notice," Dooley interrupts me, courteous as ever, "and they didn't get any kind of warning, and I need to know *why*, yesterday." He's been leaning back with his eyes shut, listening to the recording; now he thumps his chair back upright. I am glad to see that his right shoe shows no remnant of spectral blood. "Winters, get set up to run a sound spectrum check on that section of the recording, see if there's anything that even looks like a signature of aural cockpit warning tones, Stacy, you listen in with her. Liu, I want the satellite tracking maps, and rerun the FDR data from the beginning, take a close look at the flow control valve and the current in whatever bus runs the cabin-altitude and takeoff-config warning horns. Edleston, pull all the maintenance records they gave us, I want to see what that airplane was up to in the past six months, particularly with regards to the cabin pressurization system, see if they've had any issues. *Now*, people." He claps his hands.

There's a flurry of activity. I stay where I am, looking over Dooley's shoulder at the big wall screen showing the datastreams from the FedEx plane, as Liu runs it again from the beginning. It'll take a while for Winters to get set up for the sound spectrum test; I can stand here a little longer before being called over to do my job.

I'm not an expert on this part, at all, but I've been contracting with the NTSB long enough to know what a normal takeoff and climb looks like, the parameters you'd expect the instruments to stay between, that kind of shit, and this takeoff seems to be totally okay—which is strange for this type of accident. There's no weirdness anywhere in the pressurization system, flow control valve behaving normally, nothing wrong with the bleed air. The cabin pressure selector switch is correctly set according to the recording, which should have meant everything was just peachy oxygen-saturation-wise on board. Cabin pressurization issues tend to show up, obviously, at this part of the flight, while the plane is in its initial climb, but the FedEx plane had been in the air for at least a couple hours at cruising altitude before anything went hinky. Whatever was wrong with it clearly didn't mind flight level 360 that much.

Dooley's thinking. You can almost smell the burning insulation, and as I watch he takes out one of his goddamn yellow legal pads and a ballpoint pen and begins to write in his rapid chickenscratch of a personal shorthand. Nobody else can read it, which is obviously the point, and his office is stacked high with legal pads crammed full of illegible theory. I wonder *what* he's thinking.

I realize that I myself haven't thought about Captain Warner for several hours in a row. Which is kinda wonderful, in a bitter sort of way.

"Earth to Stacy," someone says. It's Winters, waiting for me to put on the serious headphones and listen in. "You want to get started sometime *today*?" She's trying to channel her boss's attitude, and it's pretty amusing, despite the subject material.

Time to go to work.

It's two A.M. before Dooley calls it quits. I'm not even sure why I'm still here, only that it seems like a better option than just kind of noping out while everybody else is hard at work. So far what they've been able to make out is … not a lot, actually. Sound-spectrum analysis of the CVR tells us what we already know: no bells, no whistles, no warning horn to tell the crew hey assholes, you're losing pressure, might wanna do something about that before you all go sleepy-bye and take a couple million dollars worth of freight with you, let alone this bucket of aerial bolts.

That's what's bugging Dooley, and it's bugging everyone else, too: so far we don't seem to have any *reason* why the warnings didn't go off. There's no dropout in electrical signal to the circuits that should have lit up those lights and horns. No obvious circuit-breaker failure. No obvious cause for the depressurization, either, which is a bigger problem.

(Again, I can't help thinking of Warner's plane standing into obvious, lethal danger with all its instruments showing green across the board, and push the thought away.)

"Okay," Dooley says, actually sounding tired rather than obnoxious, and everyone sort of looks up dully. "I want you all here bright and early tomorrow morning. Edleston's got some discrepancies in the maintenance record that I want followed up, and we haven't even gotten truly madly deeply started analyzing the goddamn data for every single part of the cabin press system. You too, Stacy, you get to play as well."

Being told to show up face to face is maybe better than getting woken up by a wee-hours phone call, but more inexplicable. "What do you need me for?"

"I don't have time or petty cash to call up the eggheads at Woods Hole and tell them to get their stable of ROVs back out there to look for the cabin press switch in what's left of the cockpit and find out what it was *actually* set to," he says.

Which is fair enough: renting the robot remote-operated-vehicle subs is far from cheap, and like most government organizations, the Board is chronically short of cash. "I want answers *now*, not in several months. That FDR data doesn't add up. I need to know what the physical switch was set to. You show up early, bring that crystal ball, tell me what I need to know, and I will even buy you a cup of shitty official NTSB coffee to show my appreciation."

"Oy vey, such a deal," I say, getting up, and *wow* I'm tired. "Truly you are the most beneficent among the ranks of the Board, Dools. I'll even bring the one with the wicked-cool pewter dragon stand, just for you."

"Sounds good. Go on, get the hell out of here."

He's sitting on the edge of one of the desks, sleeves rolled up and tie loosened, and I don't think I've ever seen the man look quite so tired. The goons and I troop out together, and the last thing I see over my shoulder is Dooley staring at the chaotic whiteboard as if all he has to do to find the answer is look hard enough at what's already there.

Alone in the parking garage, sitting behind the wheel of my beat-to-shit second-hand Corvette, I can't stop remembering what I'd heard in those last moments before the words stopped on the

CVR tape. It takes me a while to get past it. The crew had known something was wrong, but without the warning horns and lights they'd had no idea what, and it was clear that they'd gone to their deaths thinking something noxious had invaded the cockpit ventilation system; that they had been poisoned, drugged somehow, rather than killed in a stupid prosaic way by a stupid prosaic system malfunction, albeit an inexplicable one so far. I don't know which one is worse, honestly. I really don't.

When I look over, Captain Warner is sitting in the passenger seat, staring at me with the eyes he *still* hasn't got, getting his spectral blood all over my cracked upholstery. I think again of those black radar screens, of the way the instruments had lied to him, the way they had lied to our FedEx pilots, and I recall Warner's gory hand in mine and how it had felt like something had wrapped a gigantic hand of its own around his plane and *pulled* it into the storm, beyond all control.

For the first time in a great many years I wish, suddenly and hugely, that I'd never discovered my magic talents, never found this entire world, lived my whole life like a normal ordinary person who didn't have to *think* about any of this *freaky goddamn horseshit—*

Warner tilts his half a head at me, and this is just about enough to make me laugh, the screamy

kind of laughing that turns real quick into tears—
and it is only because I see through the window
past Warner's churned-meat face that Dooley
has finally emerged from the building bouncing
his car-keys in his hand that I am able to control
the desire to fucking weep. No way am I letting
Dooley see that, no matter what.

I don't know why Warner's here when I
haven't done any major significant magic shit,
but nothing else makes any sense tonight; maybe
he's drawn to the power of total and complete
fucking confusion. That could explain a whole
lot of things, in fact.

"Just don't get blood on the radio," I say to
my ghost in an unsteady voice.

I don't often have dreams. Well, not ones I can remember, so they don't count.

This might surprise you given my choice of profession. Not that I really chose it so much as failed to keep a series of more mundane jobs in a row and finally put an ad in the paper, *FREELANCE NECROMANCER*, almost as a joke. *I Talk To The Dead So You Don't Have To.*

I hadn't intended to use the whole magic thing for gainful employment. I hadn't really meant to get into it at all. Standard shitty-childhood story: I was the weird kid with no friends who was into Dragonlance and Magic cards and all that esoteric crap you soak up when you're a loner. Of course, the bullying theme went from the standard homophobic shit my name inspired to being *ooooo, Staaaaaacy, you're a* wizard, *are you gonna cast a* spell *on me??*

One day, to make them shut up, I said *yes.*

For most kids this would have been an object lesson in the unfairness of the universe, but I went home that day and I took my mom's glass paperweight from her office and sat in the middle of the garage floor staring into my half-assed crystal ball, wanting, wanting, and oh hey, would you look at that, *I saw something.* A vague and flickery something. I had no idea what I was doing and I was in the goddamn seventh grade, but there was something there, all right.

When you have a talent for this kind of thing it gets obvious pretty quick, and that kind of talent wants to be *used*, like an itch needing to be scratched. I have no idea what would have happened if the very eccentric school librarian hadn't noticed me taking out the super extra weird occult books over and over again. She took me to her office and asked me what I was doing with them, and I made up some shit about an essay for English, upon which she was the first adult who ever said the word *bullshit* to me. AKA, my first crush.

She taught me the basics of elementary magic (regular magic with a C, not a goddamn K, please and thank you). I found out that keeping it mostly secret was the easiest way to avoid awkward conversations. My mom knew I was fucking around with magic, mostly because the chalk circles in the garage were hard to erase all the way when I was done with them, but to her eternal credit she didn't tell me not to; she preferred to pay as little attention as possible to me in general, eldritch or otherwise. I don't think she really knew there was much power involved, and I didn't take steps to point it out, and that's about where the matter rested.

I never did do magic on the asshole kids who'd bullied me in middle school, other than maybe making a couple cases of acne go from moderate to volcanic; they kinda just didn't matter all that much, now that I had something more interesting than fictional D&D spells to think about. I did magic for fun, on weekends, when I needed to work off some stress: drawing my circle, practicing how to control the containment spells with little summonings until I got the hang of it, getting better, more ambitious, but still *just a hobby*. A weird and mostly secret one, but a hobby, on and off, all the way through high school, all the way through a deeply uninspired college experience. And then I can remember sitting in the parking lot of an Olive Garden at age 25 having just been fired yet *again* from yet another shitty job and thinking *fuck it, why not*. It was the only thing I was actually *good* at, so why not. People would either believe I was legit or they'd want to be fooled, and either way I'd make some cash; they'd be spending money on psychic shit regardless, so it might as well be the real thing.

The first week I got twenty calls, only about half of which were pranks. By the end of the first month, I was beginning to pay off the worst of my punitive-interest credit cards. Talking to the dead was apparently an idea whose time had come around again, especially since I was actually *capable* of doing it rather than engaging in elaborate fakery, like the mediums who advertise on local cable channels. I started a website, got a pretty decent client base going. It was only a year and a half into my new career when the NTSB called me with a clandestine proposition I found impossible to refuse, and since then shit's been pretty smooth. It has to be clandestine—remember how bent out of shape everybody got when the FBI was caught employing a psychic?—and I'm not the only supernatural-adjacent person who's working for the federal government (though we don't have a union ... yet), but none of us are allowed to talk about our jobs; we don't officially exist to the general taxpayer.

So I do magic for a living, unofficially-officially, under contract. Spirits and charms all up in the air, you name it, crystals and amulets and even some actual chanting. But I don't dream. All the strangeness and horror happens to me at the day job; I guess my brain actually goes to sleep the same time I do, rather than spending that time making up stupid shit stitched together from my subconscious. Which is why it's kind of unusual for me to find myself sitting comfortably on a cloud, thirty feet off the left wing of a 747 that seems to be hanging in space instead of doing five hundred miles an hour.

"Hi," I say to it.

"Hi yourself," says the plane. It does not have visible eyes or a mouth, but it is definitely looking at me, and I hear it quite distinctly. "I was wondering when you'd show."

"Think I must have lost the invitation." I shrug, the movement sending wisps of cloud drifting. "You want to fill me in on what exactly I'm doing on a cloud?"

"You'll figure it out," says the plane. "Remember about cockpit resource management, by the way. Too many of them don't. He'll help. He's actually your best hope, although you won't realize that for a while yet."

"Um," I say. "What the hell are you talking about, and also how are you talking in the first place?"

"Don't ask stupid questions and you won't get stupid answers," says the 747. "You'll need to pay attention, Stacy. Quite soon now you will need to pay attention."

That's not creepy in the slightest. "What do you mean *quite soon now?* What's going to happen?" Who is *he*, anyway?

The plane says nothing at all, just waggles its wings at me, and then I'm no longer sitting on a cloud but falling *through* that cloud and—

I sit up in bed, jerked out of the dream like a hooked fish, and stare into the dimness of my bedroom without really seeing it. That had been *weird*, and I do weird professionally.

The dream's still with me as I make coffee in the dark, barefoot in my boxers, the perfectly ordinary and familiar outlines of my house feeling oddly strange, as if they've been changed ever so slightly when I wasn't looking. Why I would dream about a plane talking to me is pretty obvious—it's close to what I do anyway—but why would I dream about a plane saying weird cryptic shit I was apparently expected to understand? In a way I guess it's just a reboot of the standard anxiety dream. Thanks, brain. Gotta love being made to watch yourself fuck up the job you're depended on to do.

I can't completely shake the memory of it saying *he's your best hope*, either, because who the hell is *he*? I don't have many friends, male or female, and the only other dude I work closely with on a regular basis is Wayne Dooley, which, yeah, kind of hard to fathom.

Quite soon now, it had said. *Quite soon now you will need to pay attention.*

I drive to work early, partly because I was instructed to and partly because what the hell, I'm up anyway, might as well go shower and head to the office rather than sitting around trying to psychoanalyze my own goddamn dream narratives. Especially when they're creepy as fuck. Get brownie points for showing up first.

Of course I'm not there first: Dooley's there, already at work, shirtsleeves rolled up and tie loosened, hair still perfect, looking a *little* less exhausted than the night before, but not by much. He's in his second public mode, artfully and ever-so-slightly disheveled rather than perfectly put-together, and it's pretty effective, especially since he wears the kind of tailored grey suits that expensive lawyers prefer. There's a Starbucks cup perched at his elbow which I am entirely sure is at least one third full of mocha syrup; the amount of sugar the dude consumes is impressive even by my standards, and nobody knows how he stays in shape, since the working hours he keeps don't exactly allow for a lot of time at the gym. A couple of the other investigators I've worked with suggest he's made some kind of deal with a malevolent spiritual entity, and you know what, I'd buy it.

He's watching the FDR data scrolling past on the big screen, pausing and replaying sections over and over, and I know why: this is the channel that would show any change or deviation from the normal function of the pressurization system.

"You bring it?" he asks without turning around. Straight to the point, that's the Doolmeister. Also asks unnecessary questions.

"Yeah, I brought the crystal ball," I say. "I somehow managed to remember to follow a simple instruction to transport a single object from one place to another, truly my powers are vast. Where do you want to do this?"

"You need privacy for your mumbo-jumbo, right? Use the empty office down the hall, no one will bother you. I need that cabin press selector setting, Stacy. I need it now."

"I got it," I say. I do get it: the setting of this particular knob may actually *tell* us something. If it disagrees with what's on the data recorder we have a different set of problems, but if the switch was *actually* accidentally left on MANUAL instead of AUTO we'd be able to chalk this shit up to gradual decompression due to pilot error. It's happened before. The most famous instance is Helios 522, in which the crew left the selector on MANUAL throughout the flight, failed to pay attention to the warning horns and lights telling them something was wrong, and subsequently all passed out and died, leaving the plane full of dead people flying on autopilot. The worst thing about Helios was that one flight attendant with some pilot training managed to stay conscious, using one of the cabin oxygen tanks, and the poor bastard had *just* made his way to the cockpit and gotten in touch with the ground when the plane finally ran out of gas and piled into a mountain.

(Not that he'd have been able to successfully land the thing. Aviation experts are pretty solid on that. But there might have been a fraction of a chance, instead of *hi there, mountain*.)

Some people think decompression and hypoxia is what happened to Malaysia 370, too, but nobody really knows; that one is still Cause Undetermined since they never found the main wreckage (never called yours truly in to consult on that one, since it wasn't a NTSB investigation despite the plane being American, and trust me, I'm still curious). If this FedEx thing *is* another Helios accident, cabin depressurization somehow due to pilot error without activation of the automatic warning systems, we have our answer and we can at least try to close this goddamn case, which is to be seriously desired at this point.

When I haul my heavy backpack (quartz is *rock*, an eight-inch-diameter lump of it is over twenty-five pounds, and this is why I don't transport my *really* big sphere very often) into the little office Dooley indicated, there is already something sitting on the desk. Two things. One's the piece of plane I already used as my anchor to find the black boxes, and one's an object I recognize quite well but have absolutely no idea how it got there.

An unopened Imitrex injector set, still in its safety wrapping: hail-mary migraine meds.

It's not very impressive. A small white plastic monolith that opens to reveal two doses of the stuff plus the pen you use to stab yourself. I have the same thing in my medicine cabinet at home with one of the doses already used up, after my previous astral experience with this particular wreck site.

It must belong to one of Dooley's goons; people with high-stress jobs like that often end up with migraines. They left it here by mistake, obviously; when everybody gets in at their usual time whoever it belongs to will be pleasantly surprised to have it back. Depending on how hard the current job turns out to be, I might beg on bended knee for one of the shots myself—but that's for later. Now is for the crystal.

I unwrap it from the shroud of bubble-wrap and set it on its ironic wicked-cool pewter stand shaped like a dragon—see, Dooley, I remember details—and sit down, holding the piece of fuselage in one hand and cupping the other against the dry, cool curve of the crystal itself. As always it's a minor shock when the circuit is closed, me and the crystal and the anchor-object; I jerk a little in the chair and can feel my hair trying to stand on end. But it's already working.

In the center of the ball, distorted by its curvature, is the debris-field of the dead FedEx plane. It is lit by unknown means, some dim light produced by the water itself, or maybe my astral eyes can see in the dark: don't know and don't care. Again it's not difficult to find the cockpit, the soul and center of the plane, but the extent of the damage tells me it is going to be absolute hell to find a knob the size of a Coke-bottle cap in all this mangled wreckage.

Fuck it, I think, *here goes nothing*, and push further, not just looking at the scene but pushing my mind *into* it. The version of me that's there in spirit shudders with the shock of ice-cold water for a moment before the temperature stops mattering.

I have limited time in this form, which is why I don't do it often; I'm burning up a hell of a lot of energy back in the real world, so I hurry. I know where the cabin pressure control would have been located before the crash—I'm pretty good with the dashboard layout of most of the commercial passenger jets by now—and focus on what I think is that heap of debris.

I do not, however, have any idea how long it is that I actually spend in that half-state of being, searching through the corpse of a dead plane. All I know is that my fingers close on a piece of metal I recognize, at some point, a panel with several switches and controls, and in the dim glow of the water I can see a grey knob with three settings: AUTO, ALTN, and MAN.

And *oh fuck*, I think, looking at where the knob selector is pointing, two miles down and several thousand miles away: *we* still *don't know what brought this goddamn thing down.*

I close my eyes and pull back, back out of the ocean, back out of the image of the ocean, back out of the curve of crystal and into myself much faster than I'd intended: it's a shock to feel the seat under me and the objects in my hands, real and physical and here.

It is briefly difficult to open my eyes: the light hurts like *fuck* for several seconds before they adjust, and when I can see properly I don't understand what I'm looking at.

They're all in here. The whole team of goons, and Dooley himself, all staring at me, which is when I realize I'm dripping with seawater, drenched to the skin. My head feels like it plans to explode soon, and honestly right now I wouldn't mind, it hurts so *much*.

"Uh … Stacy?" Winters asks. She looks both worried and wigged the fuck out, eyes wide behind those trendy frames. "Are you … *back* back?"

Dumb question. "Yeah. I—Dooley, you aren't gonna like this."

"I already don't like it," he says, arms folded. There's a weird look on his face that on anyone else I might have pegged as *concern*. "Any of it. Tell me anyway."

I show him instead. It sends the headache into truly astounding realms, but I show him, because talking hurts almost as bad: rewinding the memory, both hands now on the crystal, in which a kind of dim video plays. My memory.

What I saw. I'm giving them the raw footage. Easier than trying to explain.

Inside the crystal everyone can clearly see my hand close around the chunk of wreckage, pull it free, bring it up close enough to read the lettering.

The knob is set to AUTO. And we know it was set to AUTO at the time of the crash, because the pointer has left a scratch on the metal underneath it at the moment of impact.

Which means it *should* have worked. The cabin press should have been nominal. This isn't an easy pilot-error conclusion after all; they didn't forget to turn it on by mistake, or accidentally turn it off in flight. Unless they somehow managed to switch to manual, dump the press with the outflow valve, forget they'd done it, pass out from hypoxia, and then turn it back to AUTO while unconscious and/or dead, this makes no sense. The goddamn plane should have been pressurized and we *still* don't know why it wasn't.

"Welp," I say through shifting, glittering aura patterns, "I think I'm gonna have an aneurysm now, so if you guys wouldn't mind clearing out I'll get on with doing that in peace—"

"Oh for *fuck's* sweet sake," snaps Dooley, "*take the goddamn medicine*, I don't know why you didn't shoot yourself full of it *before* you started staring into the void, Stacy, you're an idiot. Here." He grabs the Imitrex I'd completely forgotten from the other end of the desk (puddles of seawater aren't doing the cheap veneer much good, someone ought to wipe that up) and slams it down in front of me.

I blink at it, and then at him. Using up this much mental energy in projection kind of leaves you slow on the uptake for a little while afterward, but eventually my thought process meanders to its conclusion: oh. The medicine was for *me*. Not left there by mistake.

For me. Dooley got hold of it for me.

I can't think about that in too much detail while the socket of my right eye is made out of white-hot iron slowly closing over my vision, so I just slowly make myself do the work of assembling and then using the injector pen. The tiny sting of the needle is imperceptible under all the rest of it.

Dooley is saying something about cots in the storage room. Tells me to get up. This hurts worse. I tell him I can't see, and he swears a lot, and then there's a hand on my shoulder and I am being walked through some kind of space, every step ringing in my head, pulsing behind my eyes, and then it is dark, and smells of dust, and Dooley lets go of me and does something clattery that sounds like unfolding a deck chair.

"You're not going to be useful for a while," he says, sounding cross about it, "so you might as well pass out here until the worst of it goes away."

The hand is back on my shoulder; he takes me over to whatever he's just assembled, tells me to sit down, and I find myself on what must be a fold-away camp bed. A horizontal surface that isn't the floor. It's perfect. I lie down on canvas that smells of dust and then I am falling through it, falling down through the floor, away from the world into soft and welcome darkness.

This time I'm not sitting on the cloud watching the plane: I'm sitting on the plane, on the leading edge of its left wing, in between where the No. 1 and 2 engine pylons are attached. We are evidently flying, as opposed to falling or sitting on the ground, but like before I don't feel any sensation of movement whatsoever. There's no 500-mph wind flattening me against the wing.

I can feel the vibration of the 747's four engines, though, two of them spinning away several feet beneath me, each of them putting out forty-something thousand pounds of thrust. Technically I should be dead in several different ways by now, or at least falling to my death, but this just feels like sitting on a very cold, vibrating park bench. My head doesn't hurt at all, which is a nice and inexplicable change.

"Pay attention," says the plane. "This is extremely basic."

I squash the urge to tell it that *it's* extremely basic: I have no idea if it might suddenly decide to let physics start being a thing again and send me tumbling off the wing into clear air. Instead I say "Um. This—might be supposed to be someone else's dream, actually." Not that it isn't a kinda cool dream, just a totally inexplicable one.

"Things don't just happen by accident," says the 747. "*You* should know that by now. You've been doing this long enough to know. You've looked up enough of the reasons why they happen, and it's never just *by accident,* it's a cascade of events. Be quiet and pay attention, and move to the top of the wing rather than its edge. Keep your feet away from the NO STEP line."

It's pointless to ask *but doesn't having me sit on your wing fuck up your aerodynamics*: clearly wherever we are those are theoretical at best. I scoot backwards until I'm sitting right on the top of the wing, its highest point, and say "Now what?"

"Slats and flaps," says the plane. "Watch this."

Underneath me machinery whines, and the leading and trailing edges of the wing extend themselves, the slats curving down from the front and the flaps tilting down from the back, and while physics doesn't seem to be working all that well in general I can immediately feel the change in lift that comes with the deeper curvature of the wing. It generates enough lift with the new configuration to allow the plane to fly at much slower speeds for takeoff and landing. I *know* this shit, it's not my first time looking at a goddamn airframe, and I say so.

"I know this," I say. "I mean, I *have* seen a couple planes take off and land before, they don't all just pile into the ground whenever I'm nearby, I know how it works, lift and drag and all that good shit."

"Ailerons," says the 747, as if I hadn't spoken, winching its wing back into the ordinary shape, and we begin to tilt gently to the right as the hinged surface at the tip of the left wing angles down. "Adjusting the angle of bank to fifteen degrees," it says, holding the bank for a few seconds before returning to level flight. It's different watching it happen than knowing intellectually how it works. "In a steep turn the stall speed increases and lift decreases, so what must you do?"

I am being quizzed by a fucking jumbo jet about Flying 101. "Uh," I say. "You'd—add power to keep speed up and raise the nose?" Stalling means losing lift; the slower you go, the less lift the wing is able to generate. Increasing the stall speed means you have to fly faster to keep flying, which means more power, but you also have to jack up the angle of attack, the nose-up/nose-down angle, to get the wing to generate more lift. I know this shit, it's impossible to work in air crash investigation without picking up the basics of aviation as it's *supposed* to work.

"More or less," says the 747. "As your bank angle increases, you decrease vertical lift; in order to maintain altitude, pull back on the stick, and increase power to compensate for drag. Now turn around and watch the horizontal stabilizer. The flat part at the base of the tail."

"I know what a horizontal stabilizer is," I say, slightly ticked, but it is actually kind of cool to watch the tabs at the back of each flat fin tilt in unison and feel the whole plane move, first raising its nose and then lowering it slightly. It's kind of cool and also it's way less upsetting than looking at Captain Warner or watching his bad death all over again.

...*This is at least the most interesting bizarre dream I've had for a while*, I think, settling more comfortably on the cold metal. *Show me.*

For once I don't wake up to the strident yelling of my alarm. It's weird: I have no idea where I am for a few moments, an unfamiliar space, stiff from lying on my side on uncushioned canvas, and then it comes back to me: Dooley's hand on my shoulder, guiding me through the blinding, fizzing aura-sparkles, unfolding the cot for me like I was one of his goons. Saying *take the goddamn medicine.*

I still can't quite wrap my head around the idea that any of them, particularly Dooley, would go to the trouble of procuring migraine meds for me, so I'm—going to put that on a shelf for further contemplation *later*. There's no sign of Warner, for once, despite how much magic I just used, and I'm gonna take that as a good thing, but there's that fragile, glassy feeling again, the one that comes after the bad headaches, and I have no idea how much time I've lost. I don't wear a watch, or keep my phone in my pocket, when I'm doing high-intensity crystal shit: it tends to turn anything electronic into an expensive brick. No way to tell how long I've been here, and no clocks on the walls. Long enough for my clothes to dry, at least; the Pacific is no longer in evidence other than a half-assed salty crust on my shirt and pants.

Gotta find out the hard way. I get up with a little bit more ease than I expected, but not much, and crack my spine in a series of little pops like pine-knots going off in a campfire. I'm *starving*, too: the projection trick burns up a hell of a lot of calories. As soon as I get out to the hallway I get my bearings. Dooley put me in the storage room at the end of the corridor, which is kind of hilarious: spare equipment *and* temporarily-offline-necromancer storage.

(I'm a little punchy. I can tell.)

And if *that*'s the main lab door down the hall, if I turn the other way I'll get to the break room with the unspeakable coffee and the vending machines, and that means dinner.

When I shuffle back into the lab, coffee mug and Twinkies in hand, the gang's all there: is *still* all there, because by the clock on the wall it's getting on for five p.m. and they've been going since seven in the morning, presumably with a brief pause to stare at me having a headache. Everyone turns to stare at me some more.

"What?" I ask after a moment, because they're still staring.

"Are you okay?" says Liu, who looks slightly more rumpled than usual, a lock of thick black hair drooping over one eye. Like the rest of Dooley's goons, he looks barely twenty, but he's gotta have at least one master's under his belt. "You looked a little … uh …"

"You *disappeared*," says Winters, her eyes wide. "Or you had disappeared already, I don't know, you weren't there, but then you suddenly *reappeared* soaking wet. Like, boom, suddenly Stacy where no Stacy was before?"

"Ah," I say. "Yeah, that happens. I'm fine, guys." I take a bite of Twinkie and close my eyes briefly in high-fructose corn syrup bliss. "We know any more about the crash?"

"We know a bunch about what it *wasn't*," says Edleston. "What do you mean, that happens? You disappear a lot?"

"Sometimes. If I push enough of myself through the levels to be able to manipulate stuff, or if I'm inside the circle and actively summoning. Still nothing on the electricals or the pressurization system?"

"Nope," says Liu. "That thing you did where you like—touched the crystal ball and there was video playing inside it, how did you do that? And how come when you came back you were all wet?"

"It's a bit damp at the bottom of the South Pacific," I say, and finish my first Twinkie. "And I can't tell you all my secrets, kids, some things are not meant for mortal investigators' ears to hear. What about the maintenance records, Edleston?"

"Wait, you were really *there*?" Winters demands. "Like you—physically went through the ball somehow?"

I am not about to launch into a lecture on Magic and You: An Introduction, so I bite off the end of the second Twinkie instead, and that is when Dooley's phone rings across the room. He's got his back to us, arms folded, ignoring me: the whiteboard is covered with his peculiar chickenscratch, slightly more legible for the benefit of other humans. He squints at the screen, listens to whoever's calling for a second or two.

"Wait. What?" he says, dead serious. The tone's impossible to mistake, and the goons return their attention to their boss just in time for him to turn around, white-faced, and say—almost shout—"Turn on CNN *right now*."

Winters scrambles for her keyboard, and a moment later the big screen lights up with the

CNN website, a bright-red LIVE: BREAKING bar across the top of the screen; under that there's a stock photo of a 737 in BrightAir livery.

At the bottom of the screen the chyron tells me what I don't want to know. *BrightAir Flight 291 Not Responding to Air Traffic Control, Terrorism Suspected: Plane Scheduled to Land at Omaha Fails to Turn to Approach Eppley Field, Continues to Fly; Local Airbase Scrambling Fighter Jets to Follow Silent Plane...*

I put the Twinkie down on the edge of a desk; I don't want it anymore. "It's not terrorism," I say, scarcely recognizing my own voice. "It's Helios. Again. This ... fucking Helios syndrome."

"The what?" asks Liu, without turning away from the screen.

"Helios 522," Dooley says, also without turning. The lines of his back are sharp, tense. "Decompression accident, back in '05. Look it up if you want details. Plane full of dead people flew on autopilot until it ran out of gas. That one was *explicable*, Stacy. That was them fucking up the cabin press selector, like our FedEx crew apparently *didn't*."

"How much you want to bet," I say, "that these guys didn't either?" That whatever fucked with the FedEx 737's pressurization controls and silenced all the alarms that might have warned them, killing that crew, is doing it again. This time to a plane full of people instead of packages.

"We're not gonna know," says Dooley, and runs a hand through his hair, disarranging it without appearing to notice. Since he's the kind of dude who mostly prides himself on looking put-together, it's not a great sign. "Until they hit the ground. So let's find out when that will be." He straightens up again. "Edleston, get on the phone to the FAA, Liu, you take the company, find out what their flight plan was, how much remaining fuel they were scheduled to land with, we can project reasonably accurately when they're going to run out of it if we know the model and how fast and high they're flying. Winters, pull this thing up on the tracking sites, check the weather, windspeed and direction. We can at least get a head start on this one."

It's not really a job you want to get a head start on. And it's not even *our* case, not yet. We're not officially supposed to be working on anything other than the FedEx crash. But it's easier to be given something to do, rather than simply stand there and watch as the seconds tick by. I don't envy those bastards in the F-16s who drew the short straw and have to fly alongside the plane: they get a front-row seat to several hundred people's bad deaths all at once. "Dooley," I say. "What do you want me to do?"

Dooley stares at me across the room, hair sticking up all over the place, and for once in his fucking life the man is lost for words.

*

In the end I just stay there with them, watching. It feels wrong to leave during something like this, even if I'm not doing anything more useful than following along with the unfolding tragedy. At one point I get up to make another pot of coffee for everyone, which I guess is better than nothing. I even bring the thing of sugar packets so Dooley can adulterate his own cup to taste, which earns me a weird look but no comment.

The flight's a nonstop from DC Reagan to Eppley Field in Omaha, operated by BrightAir, one of the no-frills low-cost carriers competing with Southwest for domestic passenger revenue. They have a pretty good safety record, as far as I know—there was a runway overrun in icing conditions at JFK a couple years ago, but that's not all that uncommon—and this is shaping up to be their first big accident. It's a 737-700, packed to its maximum of 149 passengers, all of whom are going to die if they're not already dead, and I for one really fucking hope they are. They'll shatter like glass when that thing hits the ground.

The distance from DC to Omaha is about 1,013 miles, and planes carry enough fuel to make it to their destination or alternate airport plus about 45 minutes of flying time tacked on; if they think it's likely they'll need to hold longer than that, they take off with more gas in the tank. Liu's gotten hold of BrightAir's ops people and we have a copy of Flight 291's flight plan, which includes the amount of fuel on board, the proposed altitude and airspeed, and the route it's taken from waypoint to waypoint. Edleston has the FAA's records of where the thing has actually been, based on satellite handshakes: a series of points in space.

"Look," says Winters, and points at the big screen, where the sound's turned almost all the way down. The shot of the plane is now replaced by a hairsprayed anchor, but the chyron underneath says *F-16 Fighter Jets from Iowa Air National Guard Report No Movement in Cockpit or Cabin of Stricken Flight.*

"No shit," says Liu. "You expect them to be doing the can-can down the aisle?"

It's a little weird to have someone *else* be the source of inappropriate one-liners. "Conga, not can-can," I say. "Can't do the high kicks with all those seats in the way. How much farther?"

Dooley is looking at the real-time flight tracker on a laptop, watching the green line stretch on into the emptiness of Nebraska. The altitude and airspeed are listed next to the tiny green airplane silhouette as it inches across the screen.

"At this speed, fifteen, maybe twenty more minutes," he says. "They've got to be running on fumes already, that thing's eating five thousand pounds of fuel an hour and they should have landed fifty-four minutes ago. When was the last transmission to ATC?"

"Handing off from Chicago to Minneapolis," says Edleston. "Everything about that exchange was normal, no sign of any issues. After that there's nothing on the radio."

"Show me the charts," says Dooley, and Winters pulls up the high-altitude instrument-flight-rules chart of the area in question: a white background speckled with grey circles connected by black lines and arcane sigils. The little blue crenellated line that indicates the division between one air traffic control center's airspace and the next shows the Minneapolis-Chicago border running a little way east of Des Moines; the flight plan filed by BrightAir 291 crosses the divide about a hundred and twenty-six miles east of Omaha.

"At their airspeed that's what, eighteen minutes of flight time between their last transmission and when they stopped responding?" says Dooley. "Eighteen minutes in which the cockpit decompressed enough to knock them out without them realizing—if it had been an explosive decompression they'd have declared an emergency—fuck, someone figure out how long it'd take for the cabin press on a 737 to drop that far if you set the control wrong."

Edleston grabs a dog-eared 737 manual and a notepad. It's pointless, knowing the details won't change the fact that everyone on board that plane is going to die, but doing something, anything, is better than just watching until the little green icon on the tracker screen winks out.

"They can't possibly go much further," says Dooley, almost to himself. He checks his watch. "There's no way."

We're all waiting now, almost holding our breath, almost *wanting* the icon to disappear, get it over with, end this unbearable suspense, and...it does not.

It just keeps moving, while we watch. Dooley has the tracker zoomed in far enough that we can actually see the movement of the tiny plane graphic and its altitude and airspeed, steady and slow, a testament to how goddamn fast computers have gotten and how much of what used to be ATC-only information is now available to any rando on the web: this is transponder data, transmitted and received and logged at lightning speed. It says they are still at flight level 380. Thirty-eight thousand feet.

"One hour and twenty minutes since they were supposed to land," says Liu, staring at the screen. "They must have been carrying more fuel than they declared, somehow—"

"They falsified the flight plan?" says Edleston. "They can't have, it's—why would they do that—"

"Why would they stop answering ATC?" says Dooley. "Because they planned this ahead of time, and they mean to crash the plane somewhere specific."

"So it *is* terrorism?" Winters asks. "Not the— not Stacy's syndrome thing?"

"I don't know," says Dooley, still staring at the little green plane inching its way across the screen, thirty-eight thousand feet up. "But I bet those kids in the fighter jets are getting low on gas themselves. They're going to need to refuel, and unless someone actually thought ahead, that means there's gonna be a pause before relief gets here, and if those *are* terrorists on board 291 that's when they'll make their move."

I can tell he doesn't believe it, and neither do I: it doesn't *feel* right in my gut. There's no other easy explanation, though. "What is there along that flight path that yells *terrorism target*?" I ask.

"Nothing," says Dooley, sourly. "Miles and miles of fucking Nebraska. They can terrorize some tumbleweeds, I guess, really stick it to the corrupt and greedy United States by cratering into the Dissected Till Plains. That'd sure show us, all right."

A tiny part of my brain that isn't focused on the task at hand points out that *Dissected Till Plains* would be a great name for a rock band, and how does Dooley know the official name for miles and miles of fucking Nebraska anyway?

"One forty-five," says Liu, still mesmerized, and we all fall silent; no one says anything at all.

This is impossible, we all know it's impossible, and it is happening right now in real time: Liu calls out two hours, then two hours and fifteen minutes, and I'm trying to remember how long it took Helios 522 to run out of gas when at last, with no fanfare whatsoever, the tiny airplane on the screen winks out.

Everyone lets out their breath. Dooley pinches the bridge of his nose, eyes shut, and doesn't bother to open them when his phone rings a moment later. He looks grey. "Yeah," he says into it, flat. "Understood."

The whole goon squad is looking at him a little bit like kids who aren't sure if they're going to be punished for doing something naughty. Dooley sighs. "That was the chief. Nobody had eyes on it when it went down; the flyboys had to head back for fuel and their relief hadn't caught up before it cratered, plus apparently some kind of freak storm blew up out of nowhere and fucked visibility. The Board's go-team for BrightAir is already being notified, and they're in touch with the military and local law enforcement to help search for the crash site. Not our circus, not our monkeys. Our job is the FedEx ditching, so let's get back to doing it."

Nobody else seems to have noticed a small but fascinating detail. *C'mon, Dools*, I think, through the shock—because there *is* a shock, even if I knew it was coming, that final disappearance—

you had to have picked up on that, right? Out loud I say, "You think their transponder was malfunctioning?"

"Huh?" says Dooley, and then a moment later he gets it: I can see it in his face. "Fuck. The altitude. Winters, run it back, show me right before it disappeared."

She leans over to type in a command, and the flight tracker program starts running again from about a minute before the end. He looks at it closely, then at me, and nods: an acknowledgment.

"What are we looking for?" Edleston asks.

"Watch," says Dooley, and a moment later the plane vanishes: one instant there, the next gone. "Notice anything strange?"

"The … altitude," says Winters slowly, realizing. She stands up, looking at the big screen. "It didn't change. They weren't descending."

"Which it should have done, on account of how they crashed," says Dooley. His arms are folded. "Flight level 380, steady as a rock right up until they fall off radar."

"It has to be a faulty transponder," says Liu, rolling back his chair with a creak that sounds way too loud in the rarefied lab atmosphere. "Or ratty data somewhere. I mean, it has to be, right? Like sometimes the fan speed and CPU temp monitor on my laptop sticks at a weird reading for a minute or two and then refreshes itself?"

"I find it pretty hard to imagine a circumstance under which a plane falls so fast out of the sky that it goes from thirty-eight thousand feet to the lower limit of radar coverage in less than a second," says Dooley. "Freak storm or no freak storm. I didn't see anything on the weather radar; five gets you ten that was nothing more than bullshit to cover the military flyboys' asses. They'll figure it out. Chief's assigning it to Diggs, she's good, probably the best they've got right now. Come on, people, back to work on *our* crash."

There is no way I can tell him that the freak storm that didn't show on weather-radar might actually have been a thing, because telling him that would mean talking about what killed Warner a year ago, and I still don't have a good enough explanation for that to actually mention it to Dooley. But I'm wondering if there's some kind of connection: is Warner haunting me now because the same shit is happening all over again? Did he know the BrightAir flight was going to—do whatever it's doing, and if so what the hell am I supposed to *do* about it?

It is now nearly nine pm, and I've been up since five—passing out for several hours with a migraine doesn't count, okay—and I am exhausted and heartsick and *confused* and I do not think I can be of much use at the moment, and am about to say so when Dooley sighs and sits down on the edge of a desk, pinching the bridge of his nose again. He does it when he's tired. I don't think he knows, because it makes him look startlingly vulnerable, and Dooley's not the kind of dude who does *vulnerable* on purpose. I suddenly wonder if he's got a wife or girlfriend at home, or a squadron of groupies or something, who could actually get some calories into him that aren't made out of Starbucks caramel syrup and tell him to get a couple hours of sleep. There's no wedding band, and it's kind of impossible to imagine a Mrs. Wayne Dooley, but who knows in this day and age?

"Fuck it," he says, which is also not something Dooley says all that often, at least about work. "Go home. We'll start again in the morning, I can't think straight right now."

I go to collect my crystal ball in its backpack and can't stop seeing that instant where the tiny green plane icon winked out of existence, from 380 to under the radar all at once; it's niggling at me the way shit that doesn't make sense always does. How did it crash without descending, and how the fuck had it even flown all that way on the amount of gas listed in the flight plan, and what was up with that reported storm that blew up out of nowhere and didn't show up on radar *like the one that killed Warner's plane—*

I can't think about that right now, goddamnit, the problem, okay, the real problem is *what was behind these decompressions in the first place?*

I'm so tired I barely notice Warner riding shotgun on the way home, and for the first time I think I might almost be glad of the company.

I wake up late the next morning, feeling like I've been hit by a truck, and lie there for a few minutes wondering why before remembering exactly what I'd been up to yesterday. It's been years since I did that much focused astral projection under that kind of stress, and I can't bounce back from that shit the way I did in my twenties; my mind feels *bruised*. And dull.

My phone's on the nightstand, not plugged in because apparently I was even more braindead last night when I got home than I am now; fifteen percent battery. There's a text from Dooley from two hours ago, but nothing else: *Don't come in, I don't need you today.*

Well, fuck you very much too, Doolarino. I roll back over and cover my head with the pillows and go back to sleep for another hour and a half.

*

There's nothing on the news about the BrightAir crash, which is weird. After two cups of coffee I finally find a reference to it, but no gory helicopter footage of a smoking crash site: that means it's got to be bad enough that the mainstream news sites won't air it. Great. It's just listed as missing.

(Missing works, when the plane was over water, or even over inaccessible mountainous terrain. Over *Nebraska*, not so much. It's hard to hide a smoking crater the size of a 737 on rolling prairie, even if you try.)

Not my circus, I think, *not my monkeys*, and wonder what Dooley has found on the FedEx crash that solves his problems without me around. I wish him joy of it: maybe the FDR has magically coughed up some more information explaining the depressurization, and his goons are even now typing up the preliminary report. I'm technically still on call, but right now I don't have to *do* anything about it, so maybe today I might get around to doing some of the shit I haven't had time to do lately, like mow the lawn and get groceries that don't have their names spelled wrong for legal reasons. I think I must be approximately 20% made up of various forms of *cheez*.

There's some of the other freelance work that needs to be done, as well. I check the work email (liftingtheveil@devinstacy.net) and find three pending requests to contact Loved Ones at $25 per 15-minute increments, so I fire up crystal ball number three (at six inches across, it's my daily driver, big enough for high resolution but not so massive as to suck a lot of energy) and get to work. Two of them are easy contacts, a wife and an uncle, and I get good clear messages to deliver to my clients; the third, a husband, is a real bitch to locate, and then I'm treated to a lengthy tirade about his wife's myriad infuriating habits and how remarkably glad he is to be deceased and thus delivered from them. That one I judiciously edit to emphasize that he is Happy Beyond the Veil and Wishes Her Long Life and Joy.

(That's a big part of this line of work: careful translation. You can't just go happy-assholing around literally relaying the commentary of the dead; it's a recipe for conflict and anguish and not getting paid on time. Before I hooked up with the Board, I couldn't afford that kind of fuckup, and I ended up putting a tiny clause in eight-point font on my website that I was not responsible for the content of any communication with the Departed and payment was due on delivery regardless.)

I'm at the Save-A-Lot on Annapolis Road, loading grocery bags into the Corvette, when I get a text from an old friend I haven't seen in a while now.

what are you up to? still selling out 2 the feds for fun & profit?

That's Desi all over. She's a freelance witch over in Adams-Morgan who pays the bills by running the kind of boutique that sells $400 batik caftans and hand-beaten silver jewelry, but her upstairs consulting lair is legit. She hooked me up with my main crystal supplier a while ago, and in return, I've stepped in to help her out for a weekend every now and then. Desi got me the wicked-cool pewter dragon stand for my crystal, the very best the local renaissance festival had to offer, and presented it to me with solemn gravity … which she managed to hang on to for about a minute before both of us cracked up completely. Desi's a friend.

She and I don't exactly swing in compatible directions, but she does live in the same fucked-up liminal kind of space I spend my time in, so there's shared life experience we don't need to avoid talking about. It's kinda awesome to step into her lair and get to be simply a friend, which means both *trust* and a minimum of bullshit.

yup, I reply. *The Man has swallowed my soul, I am a pawn of the capitalist machine, why?*

come be a pawn over here, I got absinthe & egg rolls & gossip

I consider it. *Don't come in, I don't need you*, Dooley had said, but as far as I'm aware the goddamn FedEx investigation is still wide open, and I do not feel like being summoned from a pleasant haze of absinthe to go scrying on short notice. Maybe once it's wrapped up I can have something approximating a life again.

Also I can't think who the fuck I might even know these days who'd be the target of gossip, and that makes me feel anthropologically ancient, and—I still *can't* ditch work and go to hang out with Desi. It's not like Dools has a ringer sitting around on some necromantic bench being like *put me in, coach, put me in, Stacy's off to have a life for a second, I promise I'll make ya proud,* even if I can practically hear the begging nasal whine.

can't, I reply to Desi, *sorry, still in the middle of a game*

u know anything about that missing plane on the news?

nope, I say. It's almost true. I know it was flying just fine until somewhere between Des Moines and Omaha, and after that it behaved extremely weirdly indeed before vanishing from radar, but this amounts to effectively nothing. Nor do I know why they haven't found the wreckage yet, which probably means that they have but are hushing it up. *not a clue on that one.*

well, hit me up when ur free, she says. *been a while*

sure has, I reply. *soon, ok?*

Soooooon, says Desi, and I suddenly miss what it was like before all this, before the Board and the reliable paycheck and the not wondering where rent money was gonna come from; the things I knew and the things I had to not know were a whole lot simpler back then. My biggest concern had been figuring out ways to tell the living what the dead wanted them to hear, and that was basically a question of spin; there was no official secrets act for freelance necromancers, and no such thing as *being on call*, and I could hang out with my goddamn friends and not have to spend time being aware of all the ways in which somebody could die on an airplane, and there weren't any grotesque dead people bleeding on my passenger seat.

On the other hand, *health insurance* just kinda has a nice ring to it.

At home I make myself a sandwich and try to answer email for all of fifteen minutes before giving up and going to search for what, if anything, is on the news. There isn't much other than what I'd seen this morning. BrightAir Flight 291 en route to Omaha from Washington, DC, is missing.

Not *lost*, not *has crashed*, but *is missing*. This time, more awake, I can't get past that phrase. A line from an old Thomas Dolby song surfaces: *one of our submarines is missing tonight/seems she ran aground on maneuvers …*

I sit back against the couch cushions and stare at the ceiling. In my peculiar field I get exposed to a lot of conspiracy theories, one way and another. I mean, a *lot*. Shit like the Bermuda Triangle and the Philadelphia Experiment, mysterious government cover-ups for supernatural disasters, alien spacecraft—the Valentich disappearance, all that kind of thing. Most of it is complete bullshit, of course, but there *are* some inexplicable events on the record, and I've experienced one of them my own self: the Mount Storm crash. That wasn't—anything ordinary, weather or pilot error or equipment failure. That one had been something else entirely, something I still don't understand. For that reason I *can* see why people still believe in the unbelievable.

What if BrightAir 291 had done the equivalent of *running aground on maneuvers*, some kind of top-secret experiment gone wrong?

In that case nobody is ever gonna find that plane, I think to myself, and put down the sandwich. *Or the hundred-forty-some people on board. Civilians. Members of the public.*

If it was an experiment, it was a horrible one.

I can remember Dooley, a couple days ago—feels like centuries—saying *lemme guess, it's the langoliers*, and I feel kind of sick at how much of my certainty is gone, now. *It's never the fucking langoliers*, I'd told him, and I hate being wrong.

I wonder what they're telling the families. How long they'd be able to keep it quiet before some outraged spouse or child or sibling goes to the press. Probably not more than a few days, maybe a week, although that's a stretch in this era of immediate mass communication.

Or maybe I'm making all this up and they're going to find the goddamn thing and Investigator Keisha Diggs and her go-team will isolate the cause of the accident and everything will be neatly squared away and I can go eat egg rolls and drink absinthe with my friend, and try to have a little less by way of overactive imagination.

I don't dream about the talkative 747 this time, and *boy* do I miss that goddamn thing when the alternative is apparently being right back in the middle of the Mount Storm crash investigation. At least Captain Warner isn't so fucking gross when he has his entire head—dude looks like your standard Middle-Aged White Airline Pilot, square-jawed, clean-cut, short-back-and-sides, little sprays of wrinkles at the corners of his eyes from a lifetime of sunglare. He's unremarkable. In the dream he's driving the plane on autopilot, hands off the control column, and this time I get to see the entire sequence from the beginning, more of it than I've ever seen before. I get to see the beginning of the storm.

It's—very much not natural. Ahead the sky is blank and clear, unlimited visibility at forty thousand feet, and in the blink of an eye clouds bloom out of nowhere, spreading through the empty air like ink in water, fast enough to look like time-lapse video. One moment there's nothing and the next there's a growing, gathering supercell, the anvil-head expanding, towering thunderheads rising up like a nuclear explosion, lenses of cloud forming over each peak as they thrust upward through the air. Storms don't *do* that, no thunderstorm can form that fast, it's not physically possible, but here this one is doing it right in front of me and Warner's forward-looking weather radar screens are completely black and clear: not even the deceptive signal-shadow readouts that imply clear air where the radar's blocked by heavy precipitation, there's simply *nothing there* to show for the huge, boiling violence of the storm we're flying into—

—and now we're into the part of this I remember from the vision Warner showed me, standing in the smoking wreckage of his plane: all over again I get to watch him staring mesmerized into the oncoming storm for much too long, until it's much too late to turn—he tries, of course he tries, once the spell's broken, but he's only just begun the turn when the plane slams into the cloud—

I jerk awake, breathing hard, and there the fucker is standing at the foot of the bed and bleeding at me. In the dark he's visible because he's ripping off the Force-ghost thing from *Star Wars*, every feature—or lack thereof—outlined in faint blue light. It doesn't do him any favors.

"What do you *want?*" I yell at him. "What the fuck do you *want* from me? I don't know what that was, I didn't know what it was when you *showed me the first time*, I still have no clue what killed your plane, okay?"

It is not okay and I know it, and I cover my face with my hands and flop back against the pillows so as not to see him slowly shake what's left of his head. When I peek through my fingers he's gone, without even leaving ectoplasm on the duvet, and there is yet again no chance in hell I'm getting back to sleep before morning.

After a while I roll out of bed and go to make coffee in the pre-dawn darkness. Still nothing from Dooley, either via text or email, and— standing at the sink, watching the sky fade from ultramarine through green to lemon-pale—I have abruptly had enough of this bullshit. I don't know why Warner seems to have glommed on to me, but it's a major drag and I am pretty sure it's affecting my performance, and I need to *do* something about it. Without Warner taking up my mental run-time, who knows, maybe I might have been able to find something useful in the FedEx CVR recording instead of sitting there like an idiot and listening to three people die.

It's still way too early to text Desi: she doesn't exactly rise with the sun, and I'm not that kind of asshole. I email her instead:

hey, if you got time and absinthe today I'll bring the egg rolls, I got a favor to ask

I feel better almost at once when I hit *send*. There's relief in finally admitting I might be in over my head on this one. I've always been out on my own, my whole life, that's never not been true, and acknowledging that I need help isn't the easiest thing in the world for me ... but God, it'd be nice to *not* be the only one dealing with Captain Warner.

I get a text around eleven-thirty, *eddie's please :) :) :)*, and it only takes me about half an hour to get into the city and pick up takeout from Desi's favorite Chinese place. Her magic shop's on 18th, sandwiched between a tattoo place and an art gallery. I've never stepped into either. My battered second-hand Corvette doesn't look out of place parked out front. She has the predictably expensive batik caftans displayed in the store window along with a selection of clunky sterling jewelry, but there's a discreet little moon and stars in purple neon up in one corner of the window: visual shorthand for psychic shit available within.

(Purple neon *always* means psychic shit. I don't know when that happened, but it's universal: you see a purple neon sign, it's going to be advertising some kind of tarot or crystal or palm-reading service, every time. Desi's display is kind of a balancing act, aimed to appeal to the ordinary punters and the more specialized clients at once.)

She's with a customer when I come in, fragrant paper bags in hand, and gives me a smile over her shoulder. As usual, she's wearing her own merchandise, and this is one of the reasons people are so eager to hand her wads of cash; there should be a little warning label on the inside of her dresses that says *you will never look as good in this as Desi Serensky does*.

The customer departs, less $389.95, and Desi flips the sign on the door to CLOSED. "Jesus, *that* took forever," she says. "Come upstairs and show me what you've brought and tell me all about it, have you finally fallen in love with somebody unsuitable?"

"Nope." I hand her the bags. "I got myself a ghost problem."

"*You* have ghost problems?"

"Just one, but he's kinda significant, though. Also I'm having weird dreams."

"You totally need absinthe," says Desi, and nods toward the stairs.

Her upstairs apartment is a comfortably cluttered lair; the front room where she sees clients features a shawl-draped table supporting a crystal ball, and the rest of it is furnished with cushions and rugs and low tables. She clears off one of these, setting aside a tall and impressive brass hookah, and starts opening takeout cartons. "Start from the beginning."

So I do, in between stuffing my face. I tell her about the Mount Storm crash investigation, about what I'd seen and felt and heard, and how I'd had to fudge the account I gave to Dooley of what actually killed the plane. Instead of the promised absinthe she's cracked a couple of beers, and that kind of helps with the story-telling part.

"So ever since then I've seen him, now and then, when I do pretty heavy magic—but it's getting more frequent. A *lot* more frequent. Last night I dreamed about the crash and he was there when I woke up, and—he wants something, obviously he wants answers, or—I dunno, closure—and I can't give it to him. And it's kinda fucking up my day job, to be honest, so I was hoping you'd be able to help. Or at least tell me what to do about it."

Desi has watched me evenly, grey eyes narrowed in thought, throughout this little narrative. She has a couple of lacquered chopsticks shoved through the messy red knot of her hair, much nicer than the cheap disposable takeaway version she's using to eat.

"When you say fucking up your day job," she says, fishing around in the fried rice for a piece of chicken. "Do you mean you're not able to *do* the tricks, the projection and so on?"

"I did it just fine, except for the killer migraine afterward," I tell her. "Went all the way out to the bottom of the Pacific to find a knob the size of a soda bottle cap. Not that it did any good: we still don't know what the hell happened to the FedEx plane. Last I heard, anyway. Dooley's been radio silent."

"And no one else can see this guy?"

"Either they can't see him or they don't think a six-foot-tall dead dude with no face is worth remarking upon," I say, and bite off the end of an egg roll. "I'm gonna go for option number one. Then again these people are severely psychically un-sensitive, I think it's a requirement for NTSB investigators, right after lacking a sense of humor."

"This is the first time you've *dreamed* specifically about him?" She's all business. It's kind of reassuring and kind of really not.

"I think so? Maybe. Also there's this jumbo jet that talks to me."

"Huh," says Desi. "What does it say?"

"Stuff about cockpit resource management and how to use ailerons." I shrug. "What do you think the deal is with Warner?"

"Can't tell without doing an actual reading. Which I'm gonna, as soon as I'm done eating lunch. You want the rest of that chicken?"

*

Half of what Desi does for her clients is stage-direction bullshit: the incense, the draperies, the flowing outfit and eye makeup; the other half is solid utilitarian scrying. It looks like what I do when I Draw Aside the Veil and play messenger to the dead, but she's not using her talents for posthumous communication, exactly. She's visualizing the part of me that exists on a different plane of reality: my pneumic signature. It helps some people to think of it as a soul. Desi's way better at it than I am, and it's practically impossible to do on your own self, but it always feels a little weird to be observed at this level. There's no one else I'd trust to do this to me, except her, and I still am not looking forward to it one bit: it's like a spiritual colonoscopy.

She's fetched one of her crystals and set it on the low table between us, now clear of takeout containers, and she has my hands in hers, her grip cool and strong. "Ready?"

"Do it," I say, and a moment later shut my eyes—not fast enough to miss the point where the chopsticks in her hair are tossed free as the whole two-foot red length of it unwinds and stands out straight from her head in an aureole: *damn* she's putting a lot of energy into this. More than I've ever seen her use on a client. It's like touching a Van de Graaff generator, the humming crackling shimmer-sense of some vast charge building up—the crystal between us is glowing bright enough that I can sense it even through my eyelids—

—I can *feel* her probing at the edges of me, gentle but inescapably intrusive, examining me the way Dooley's metallurgist goons examine bits of wreckage, looking for any deviation from the norm, any tiny cracks that might solve a greater mystery, anything that could explain what the actual hell is going on—she's way down deep into the very nitty-gritty of what makes me *me* and I don't really want to think about that too hard because I don't necessarily want to know—God that feeling of being explored, *nibbled at* by someone else's mind is fucking hard to deal with even if you know it's coming—

—in fact she's deep enough that the sudden jangling clamor of my phone *jerks* her back out of me, a sudden static-shock as the built-up energy discharges all at once, taking both our breath away in an instant of sharp and sickening vertigo, and it has to ring again twice before I can get my shit together enough to fish it out of my pocket and stare at the screen.

Dooley.

Fuck, I think, and lift the phone to my ear, still mentally ringing with the shock of that abrupt withdrawal. It feels the way unexpected pressure changes do, disorienting, like not just my ears but the whole inside of my *head* needs to pop. "Hello?"

"Stacy," Dooley snaps, "drop whatever you're doing and get your ass over here *right the fuck now*."

"What's—did something happen?" I facepalm: it's the dumbest question I've asked in a long time. Desi is staring at me with an unreadable expression and slowly twisting her hair back up into its knot. There are still tiny sparks crawling in it here and there.

"*Get over here*," Dooley repeats, and the line goes dead.

Driving in DC is shit even when you haven't just had your pneumic signature *twanged* on top of a 7% Imperial IPA, and I am not sure *enough* that Dooley would pull a string or two to get me out of traffic court to take a bunch of risks; it takes me a while to get to the office.

Desi hadn't said much before I left; just that she'd gotten some useful information—not what it was, of course—and she'd work on analyzing my problem and get back to me. I hadn't had the presence of mind to ask her any sensible questions, just thanks and goodbye, before I ran out the door.

The whole way down to L'Enfant Plaza in the Corvette I'm wondering what the fuck they could have found that'd make him summon me in such an all-fired hurry, and none of the options seem to make sense. No one would bother to get me there in person just to acknowledge that the team's discovered the reason our FedEx 737 took a dive, right? All Dooley'd have to do is *say so* on the phone, without the weird hanging-up drama—

—and if it's the other one that's *not* ours, the *missing* BrightAir flight, okay, either it's no longer missing or some kind of explanation has been found, and again, why the hell would they need me there for that? I'm a consultant of last resort, *contingency communications specialist*, not so much a regular member of the team. Unless they've found it in lots of little pieces and need me to have a chat with the ex-pilots to find out why, but Dooley would have *said* so, said *we got one*, it's the phrase he always uses when he summons me to commune with the dead. I don't think it's crashed. Not yet.

(Where the hell could a 737 go *missing* over Nebraska, I can't help thinking again, and don't like any of the options that come to mind, either. Some kind of fucked-up plot to steal the plane, for reason or reasons unknown; alien abduction; the world's shittiest prank?)

When I get there the whole team is in the middle of frenzied activity. Winters has what looks like live cable news up on the big screen, split to show that plus the real-time flight tracking software; Dooley and Liu are on various phones; Edleston is typing rapidly on a couple of laptops at once. I'm leaning in the doorway watching them, which is why it takes me a few seconds to twig what's weird about the show Winters is playing.

"Um," I say, looking up at the screen. "Is that recorded footage?"

Dooley turns to stare at me. "*There* you are, Jesus Christ, I said *right away* not *whenever you get around to it*, Stacy."

"Traffic," I say, still watching the screen. "What the hell is going on?"

"Well, we were kind of hoping *you* might be able to fill *us* in on that aspect of this particular situation, actually," he says, enunciating with irritated clarity. "No. That's live. Satellite feed. It's not some kind of signal intrusion, either, nobody's beaming this in to fuck with us. What you see is what you get."

"So that *is* BrightAir 291," I say. I guess our FedEx crash is on the back burner once again. "A little off its original flight path. Thirty-eight thousand feet over the ... uh ... Indian Ocean. Zipping along at four hundred and forty miles per hour."

"Sure looks that way to me," says Dooley. "Remember what happened when it disappeared?"

"Vividly," I say. "The funky part was how it just winked off of radar without apparently bothering to descend, like, at all."

"That was the last anybody saw of it until about forty-five minutes ago," says Dooley. "The news said it was *missing*, which—is actually one hundred percent true, for once. There wasn't a crash site. Nobody could find a goddamn trace of the thing—Diggs and her team grid-searched half of fucking Nebraska for the slightest hint of debris, and there's simply nothing there to be found. If it crashed, it crashed *real* gentle-like and was promptly hidden away in some secret hangar somewhere."

"You don't believe that," I say.

"Nah. I don't. I don't know what the hell to believe, other than what I'm seeing."

It might be the first time I've heard Dooley admit any such thing. "So—what, it just randomly popped up again? Dropped out of hyperspace?"

"Indonesian early-warning radar picked up a strange signal—" he checks his watch "—forty minutes ago, and their ATC registered the BrightAir flight's transponder shortly afterward, but all attempts to make contact with the plane have failed. It's heading southwest over the Indian Ocean on what our projections suggest is basically a circumnavigational path based on their original flight direction."

"Like they just kept going over Omaha and round the other side of the world on that vector," says Edleston, pulling up an animation of the turning globe of the Earth. "It's not deviating based on weather or other traffic or anything, it's just—flying straight. The military's a little freaked out."

"More than a little," says Dooley. "I'm not looking forward to the part where it starts to approach the United States again."

"Also it's screwing with ATC," says Liu, putting down the phone. "So far there's been one near-miss due to this thing randomly appearing in controlled airspace where other flights are being vectored. If it stays on its current path, control can route traffic around it, but—there's no guarantee with this. We don't know what's responsible."

"We don't know what's *driving*," says Dooley, turning to me. "That's where you come in."

"Me?" I say. "The hell am I supposed to be able to do?"

"We got BrightAir to overnight us a bunch of stuff from that plane, things that got switched out during maintenance checks but belong to that airframe. I want you to try your crystal-ball trick on that stuff and see if we can get a look inside that plane."

Shit. "I can *try*," I tell him, "but—it's going to be vague as hell if I do get anything, at this distance and with that much of a remove from the plane itself." I've never tried it with an aircraft that wasn't on the ground, or at the bottom of a major body of water. "I need my good crystal, it's back at home—give me a couple hours to get there and back again—"

"Not acceptable," says Dooley. "We got no idea how long we have before that thing goes bye-

bye again. I'm authorizing priority transportation."
He picks up the phone again and gives a series
of orders, and—despite everything, despite how
I already kind of have a headache even before I
do my trick, it's still just a little bit cool that I'm
gonna get to ride in back of a NTSB Tahoe with
the lights and sirens blazing like I'm some kind
of extra-corrupt cabinet secretary.

Hey, you take it anywhere you can get it,
these days.

In fact we're exactly eighteen minutes too late.
When I get back to the lab, out of breath, the
entire team looks like somebody just shot their
collective grandmother, and on all the screens,
where the freaky plane had been tracing its neat and
predetermined flight path, there is precisely dick.

"How long?" I ask, and Liu tells me, and then
there is a little bit more silence.

Dooley is standing with his arms folded,
staring up at the empty screen. He looks
exhausted, and more than a little fragile, which
is not something I had tended to associate with
him before the past couple of days. Obnoxious,
yes, irritable, sure, but not *fragile*. I wonder again
whether there's a Mrs. Dooley somewhere, or
if he just plugs himself in at night to recharge.

He turns to me. "Stacy."

"Yo," I say.

"The BrightAir crap is in that box on the far table," he says. "See if you can find out where that plane has gone. Anything. Any data at all."

I hadn't been confident about my ability to scry the thing when it was physically present; I know damn well I won't be able to see into *other universes*, or wherever this thing keeps disappearing to, but—doing something is better than doing nothing, and hey, I lugged the crystal all the way back here, after all. I go to fetch the box, heading for the little office I'd used before when I searched for the cabin press selector knob on the FedEx plane, and the last thing I see on the main screen is some witty asshole from one of the cable networks talking about the Flying Dutchman: *it should have been a KLM flight.*

It's funny, in a terrible way. I close the little office door, set the crystal on its stand, and rummage through the box of BrightAir parts to find something sufficiently complex and important to use as a focative point. Most of it's junk, faulty instruments or control knobs the maintenance crew had switched out at some point or another, but underneath a damaged breaker panel I hit the jackpot: the power control unit servo valve that works the 737's rudder.

These fucking things killed a bunch of people back in the nineties before the Board twigged what was going on: after spending a while freezing its ass off at high altitude, if hot hydraulic fluid got

pumped through the valve to push the rudder left
or right, it could jam. And jam in a particularly
weird way, not just sticking but sometimes
reversing, sending the rudder all the way hardover
to its limit in the wrong direction, which as you
can imagine led to more than one plane auguring
upside-down into the ground. Parker Hannifin,
the company that made the PCU, redesigned the
thing so it was less lethal, and the saga of the 737
rudder hardovers came to an end, but these things
are still definitely *important*. Significant. Precisely
the right type of artifact for someone such as
myself to use as a scrying focus. Presumably this
one reached the end of its useful lifespan, or broke
and was replaced; I have no way of knowing why
they took it off the plane. It doesn't matter. Only
the link signifies.

I settle down, valve in hand, and cup my other
hand to the cold curve of the crystal—satisfying, as
always, that perfect pregnant swell—and prepare
to give myself a headache all over again, and—

—not a goddamn thing happens. I might as
well be touching a can of Coke instead of the PCU
for all the image I can get. The crystal doesn't
even display blankness; it remains completely
clear. Could be a big-ass lump of Lucite instead
of pneumically polarized quartz.

I put the PCU valve down, not without regret,
and proceed to try all the rest of the artifacts in
the box. Nothing whatsoever. Wherever that

plane has gone, my brand of magic is apparently incapable of following. It feels...*bad*, like it's me that's failing, like I'm not trying hard enough, but there's literally nothing I can do that makes the crystal so much as flicker.

When I look up from the desk Warner is there, *right there* watching me, and I glare at him, sitting back in the chair. "The hell do you *want?*"

Silence. The blood makes no sound as it drips to the floor. Then, in the first concrete and possibly even helpful thing he's ever done since he started haunting me, Warner reaches out one hand and points what's left of his finger at the PCU valve I'd tried first.

"What about it? It doesn't work, none of this shit works. I can't get even a hint of a return."

More silence. He doesn't move, doesn't stop pointing at the thing, and after a moment I pick it up again: a metal cylinder about seven inches long and three in diameter, with a smaller cylinder inside it sticking out at one end. When I look up again, he's gone, without leaving spectral bloodstains on the linoleum; you have to give the asshole credit for some manners, I suppose.

I wrap the crystal up in its protective bubble wrap and settle it back into my backpack, and after a moment add the PCU. I might as well have the thing with me in case the Flying Not-Dutchman decides to show up again.

I have a feeling that it will.

*

I have to say I'm kind of impressed by how well Dooley's goons are taking this whole situation, to be honest. I'm peculiarly well suited to believe the unbelievable, on account of I spend a lot of my time talking to dead people, but these kids are scientists; it's got to be at least a little challenging to go from Everything Makes Sense to What the Actual Fuck without much notice. They seem to have made the transition remarkably smoothly. Dooley himself is also apparently not actually losing his shit regarding the fact that things have gone all supernatural, which is also pretty impressive given the fact that he's the most annoyingly rational person I know. Maybe someone put Xanax in the coffee machine.

I'd gone back to the lab and told them the crystal ball was no go, and Dooley told me to go home, which honestly I didn't argue with; the whole weird abortive little episode with Desi earlier had been kind of draining, and I haven't been getting that much quality sleep what with talking planes and Warner the Amazing Faceless Companion and all. I'm settled on the couch with beer and pizza, flicking through the TV channels to find something worth watching, when Desi texts me.

stace i figured out what the deal is w/ur ghost pilot

All there is on TV is news, basically the same shit across every channel. I text her back: *how come he won't leave me alone?*

took me a while to get it, she says. *kind of a forest vs trees thing*

That's not ominous in the least. *spill already,* I reply.

so when u went out there to west virginia or wherever he crashed & met him, he took u witchwalking, she says. *thats a technical term btw*

The bit where I got to see his memories, yeah, I say. *his fucking weirdass memories that I had to cover up in the report*

yeah that, idk if he knew he was doing it but prob not anyway that whole experience kind of

She breaks off and a moment later, before I can reply, adds *stapled u guys together*

I stare at the screen. *stapled,* I repeat.

also technical term. ur pneumic signatures r basically linked 2gether

Well, that's just fucking *peachy*. I pause for a moment before texting her back. *so wtf do I do about it, can we get UNstapled*

yeah it just will take some work & u wont like it, in the meantime he means u no harm, hes showing up whenever u do major magic shit bc it kinda sorta summons him or like gets his attention, just try 2 ignore i guess?

jesus christ i don't need this, I reply, and get a string of sadface emojis in return; I am about to ask her for an actual appointment to deal with the problem when she adds *g2g sorry customer* and I know she's unavailable for at least the next half an hour.

Fucking great. Warner and Stacy, sitting in a tree, I think, and drop the phone on the couch beside me, returning my attention to the TV. Still just wall-to-wall news.

It's almost word for word across networks. *MYSTERIOUS PLANE REAPPEARS BRIEFLY. BRIGHTAIR FLIGHT 291, WHICH DISAPPEARED OVER NEBRASKA A DAY AGO, WAS SPOTTED CRUISING OVER THE INDIAN OCEAN FOR SEVERAL HOURS BEFORE DISAPPEARING ONCE MORE. CONTACT WITH THE AIRCRAFT HAS BEEN CONTINUOUSLY ATTEMPTED WITHOUT SUCCESS. AVIATION EXPERTS ARE FLUMMOXED.*

I just bet they are. CNN has good old Greg Feith on—entirely silver up top now but still annoyingly handsome—asking him unanswerable questions and waving a model of the 737 around. They get to "and how is the airplane capable of flying when it should have run out of gas a long time ago?" and Feith is in the middle of trying to look patient when they cut to the Board's headquarters: the Chief is giving the world's least informative press conference, and right now I don't envy him one little tiny bit.

I've got the PCU valve from the BrightAir plane beside me on the couch, for some reason. It feels weirdly necessary, or comforting, or something, to have it close, as if it could somehow give me answers without me being the one to ask. I can't quite forget Warner standing there in the office, pointing at it, with the drips of spectral blood from his fingertip falling with tiny silent splats on the desk, knowing that none of Dooley's kids would be able to see either the finger or the blood. Sometimes this gig is so fucking *lonely* it makes you kind of sick, you know?

The Chief is parroting the only talking points the Board leadership has apparently been able to come up with: investigation is ongoing, no evidence that terrorist activity is behind the strange behavior of the airplane, they are working with the company and with ATC worldwide to ensure that the safety of passenger air travel is not compromised by this situation. I'm kind of glazing over when on the screen there's a sudden disturbance, reporters and Board agents alike reaching for their phones or touching earpieces; the Chief falters in his narrative, and I don't need to wait for Dooley's call a minute later to know what's happened. Under my fingers the BrightAir PCU does not exactly vibrate but *thrums*, once, a quick wash of heat through the metal, there and gone again, and I don't answer Dooley at once because I am off the couch and running for my fucking crystal ball.

I don't bother with the stand, either, just taking the thing back to the couch with me and settling it in my lap, its weight on my thighs heavy enough to be uncomfortable, but nothing matters right now other than getting through to that plane. I do manage to thumb speaker on my phone and Dooley's voice, flat with distortion, quacks at me. "—Stacy, fucking pick up, the thing's back, it's fucking back, get online with your shit and tell me what's going on—"

"Way ahead of you, Dools," I tell him, and then my hand closes around the PCU valve and the circuit is complete and my living-room blanks out instantly, shock-fast, and is replaced by the familiar cockpit of a 737.

The completely *empty* cockpit.

There's no pilot. No first officer, no flight engineer, nobody deadheading. No brave yet ineffective flight attendants like the poor motherfucker on board Helios 522 who might have had a chance at landing the thing if he hadn't run out of gas. Nobody. No debris on the seats, either, no joint-replacements or gold tooth-fillings or still-clasped wristwatches lying around to give witness to the people they had once belonged to. It's just empty.

And it's flying. The instruments are green across the board except the cabin altitude and takeoff config warning lights, showing the cabin's lost pressurization: no surprise there, although the frost on the windows is long gone by now, sublimated away. Sunlight pours over the instrument panels, and I can see past dancing motes of dust that nothing is visibly wrong. It's reading close to the takeoff fuel weight on the wing tanks, the configuration it'd have shown on leaving Washington National. Forward-looking radar shows no bothersome weather up ahead. Autopilot's engaged, course set. Altimeters on both the captain's and first officer's sides show 38,000 feet, knots indicated airspeed is a hair over 440. All systems fucking nominal save the cabin press and I am staring out the front windows at the empty glory of sky with the sea a long way below—it's still over the Indian Ocean but heading for landfall if it's going to continue its circumnavigation of the globe on this same path and *everything is wrong* even if the boards show almost everything is right—

I know intellectually how goddamn fast midair collisions between airliners at cruise speed can occur: both parties are traveling at hundreds of miles an hour, and without sufficient warning time it is practically impossible for two planes at the same flight level on intersecting trajectories to take evasive action, which is why there are so many passive traffic-avoidance systems built into every new and refurbished airliner that's fit to fly. But it is still out of absolutely fucking *nowhere* when the red-and-white Qantas plane flashes past my windows less than a hundred feet below, sending the BrightAir 737 yawing violently to the left with the force of its slipstream. My aircraft's TCAS—traffic collision avoidance system—didn't even squeak, gave no warning whatsoever. It's close enough that for a flash of a second I thought I could actually see into the other plane's cockpit, get a glimpse of a pale oval with dark patches—a face, blank with horror—and then my plane rights itself and settles back to level flight.

That was too fucking close. I'm shaking, nauseated with adrenaline, not really aware of how tight I'm clutching the PCU valve in my right hand. Slowly, through the pounding of my own heart, I can begin to hear the quacking of a voice nearby: Dooley, still on the phone. It's taken only a few seconds for the entire sequence to play out. "—Stacy, for fuck's sake are you even still there—"

"I'm here," I say, hating how I sound, nausea warm in my throat. "Dooley, this thing just nearly plowed right into a Qantas at four hundred forty knots. I saw it."

"Are you sure?" he demands.

"Fuck you, *yes* I'm sure," I snap. "I was *there*, okay? I'm—I'm still there—"

An idea occurs to me, and I stop talking to him entirely, closing my fingers tighter around the crystal and the PCU valve and *pushing* myself through, the way I'd pushed through to the Pacific to find the remains of the FedEx plane's press control knob, what feels like a lifetime ago. It hurts, the way opening your eyes underwater hurts, but I do it anyway, leaning through to reach for the control column on the right side of the cockpit, and find that my fingers can close on the hard plastic of the first officer's handgrips; that, with a little more pressure, I can turn the yoke ever so slightly.

And the plane tips. Just a little, but the left wing dips down in response to my input. When I let go, it rights itself, without fuss or fanfare, resuming level flight—but it *responded*, for that space of a few seconds.

If I can do it through projection, it can *be* done in real life.

All of a sudden the fucking dreams snap into focus. Sitting on the wing and listening to that completely ordinary and completely impossible voice chatting on about flight controls.

Stapled, I think. *He took you witchwalking and your pneumic signatures are linked ... when you do magic it summons him.*

He's actually your best hope, although you won't realize that for a while yet.

Warner, silently pointing at the PCU valve, drops of spectral blood dripping from his fingertip. Standing at the foot of my bed. Staring at me from my passenger seat: *what do you want?*

Quite soon now you will need to pay attention.

It clicks.

I let go of the PCU and the vision blanks out instantly, a ringing silence and blackness in my mind, and it takes a moment or two before the familiar shapes of my living-room begin to take shape once more, rising back out of that blackness.

Dooley is *still* on the phone, bless him, and I pick it up in shaking fingers and cut him off in mid-expostulation.

"Dools," I say. "I know what has to happen. I know what we have to do."

"What the fuck are you talking about, *we*," Dooley demands. His voice has a weird wavering high note in it I don't remember hearing before. It's almost interesting, or it would be if I didn't feel so deadly fucking sick and scared and *tired*.

"Not you," I qualify, thinking again *stapled*, thinking *linked*. "But I think I do have to."

"Do *what?*"

"Get on board that plane," I tell him, and wish to all the fucking gods that never were that I'd never, ever opened a spellbook; that I'd never felt the beginning pull of magic as a stupid kid, too young to know better, too excited to know how bad an idea it was; that I'd never, ever taken this fucking job in the first place, never found myself in Mount Storm, West Virginia, never faced a dead pilot and taken his hand in the smoldering wreckage of his plane and been drawn into a vision of hundreds of people's bad death, never had my soul-self knotted up with someone else's in a dream-state I can't fix. That this could be *someone else's problem*, anyone else in the goddamn universe, other than my own.

"... I'd ask are you sure," says Dooley, sounding like someone's just punched him pretty hard, "but I think we're all beyond that, right now. Get down here. I'll make some calls."

"Ten-four." I reach blindly for the phone, managing to hang up without knocking it on the floor and cover my face with my hands for a long, long moment, trying to remember just what the fuck the plane had said to me, back in the dream. Flaps and slats. Ailerons. And cockpit resource management. That I'd have to pay attention. That *he'd help*.

And now he's here: Warner, faceless and bloody. I know without turning around that he's standing behind the couch, quite close. Close enough to touch, if he had corporeal form. That he's been here the whole time I was on the plane, focused through the crystal. Watching me.

Stapled, Desi had said. *Witchwalking.*

I'm going to have to find out for myself what exactly that shit means.

5

Turns out it wasn't just that Qantas that the BrightAir nearly plowed right into in midair. Turns out, in fact, there were three near-misses that time before the fucking thing vanished from radar all over again, and one of them was so close that the other plane actually sustained damage from the turbulence and the evasive action the pilots had to take. I have it on good authority that at least two air-traffic controllers are on emergency personal leave right now, and fuck knows when or if they're going to have the nerve to get back behind the radar screen with that kind of mental trauma hanging over them. Remember John Cusack in *Pushing Tin*? I don't know how those ATC assholes even have the guts to go to work when everything's going hunky-dory, with that responsibility over their heads, hundreds and hundreds of people going hundreds of miles an hour in different directions all needing to be vectored and separated and guided and steered to where they're going, but a rogue 737 merrily popping in and out of existence screwing everything up is more than anyone could be expected to handle.

And they can't shoot it down. The optics on that would be unspeakable. Back when Helios 522 stopped responding to ATC, in 2005, I think the Greek air force actually did think about it pretty seriously—but this is a North American carrier, in the sight of the entire world, and there were at one point a bunch of American citizens on board that bus, and nobody who votes to shoot it out of the sky is going to have a job come the next election. So there's got to be another way to put it on the ground, right? Right. There has to be a way, and I know what it is.

I keep telling myself this. All the way up in the fucking air tanker I keep telling myself this.

Convincing Dooley I needed to get up there had been impossible until I gave up with the rational shit and offered him the big old truth-bombs: I'm basing this on a ghost and on a dream, nothing more substantial than that, but maybe, just maybe, the only thing that can land a ghost plane is a ghost *pilot* and I just happen to have one of those on hand; I am not going to send someone *else* up there to take control of a rogue phantom aircraft that might just stop existing at any moment and take them with it off into the dimension of the fucking langoliers, or wherever this thing keeps disappearing to. I have to do it myself because I'm the only one with a ghost pilot of my very own.

Back in L'Enfant Plaza he'd leaned against his desk, pinching the bridge of his nose between thumb and forefinger, for a long time, before agreeing.

Good, I'd said, *I need to get up there somehow—the Air Force's gotta have something that can somehow rendezvous with that thing, right? It's depressurized, I should be able to open the door to get inside, and I know that when I get there I'll have help to land it—*

Stacy, you are many things, including an insubordinate asshole, we know this to be true, Dooley had told me, *but there is no way I am going to let you do this incredibly stupid stunt alone.*

I won't be *alone, that's my point*, I told him.

You're going to need someone else to help, he said, *someone who isn't dead, who actually exists outside your goddamn head, in the real world, and knows what the fuck they're talking about*, and then he'd turned away from me, covering his face for a moment, and reached for his phone— and now, as I try really hard to not think about what I'm about to do, it's a weird and unexpected comfort to find that Chief Investigator Wayne Dooley gets exactly as airsick as I do in the back of a goddamn Stratotanker.

I'd tried to talk him out of it. Tried pretty hard, because who wants their *boss* tagging along on a fucked-up mission as impossible as this one, especially if you don't know you're coming back? I might as well have done interpretive dance at him: Dooley had insisted, with that rock-hard *determination* that characterizes the man. He'd said something about responsibility, about not sending someone to go do something he wouldn't do himself, which came as something of a shock—and then I thought of the Imitrex on the table, and the hand on my shoulder, guiding me through blinding sparkles, and, okay, maybe I should give the guy a shred or two more credit for humanity. It's weird to think about, so I'm trying not to, and the fucking plane we're on is making *that* easy.

It's only because this is *so* far beyond anything the armed forces have ever been called upon to deal with, and because there's the general sense that the CIA is behind it—or someone even worse than the CIA, if you can imagine—that Dooley's demands got passed up the chain as fast as they did. Within a few hours of his original call he and I and my storied goddamn crystal ball (and my PCU valve, can't forget that) were on our way to Andrews AFB, a place I had never in my life anticipated visiting.

I just about had time to call Desi in the car on the way over, mostly to tell her that I was off

to go do secret shit for the government and might
not be back, in which case she was welcome to
my Corvette and all the occult junk in my garage.
I could tell she had a lot more she wanted to say
about the whole situation, particularly about my
connection with Warner, but there wasn't much
time, and anyway I didn't feel like having deep
meaningful conversations with Dooley sitting
right there emanating Not-Pleased about the
entire deal. (He'd said goodbye to his goons, and I
was not imagining it when I saw how worried they
were: hero-worship's weird.) If we get through
this it is Desi's turn to get the takeout, that's all
I know, and I might even invite Dools and the
squad to join us in an egg roll.

Right now I'm bouncing round in the back
of this goddamn bucket of bolts somewhere over
Nebraska and trying not to hurl on anything
that might compromise national security, and
wondering exactly where I lost control of my life
and if there's anything I could have done about it
at the time. We're up here with a bunch of guys
from the Air Force who look right out of central
casting and probably have cool-as-shit call signs
and get in trouble for buzzing the tower all the
time, but it is super evident how much they are
not thrilled at having to prepare a couple of
fucking ignorant unfit *civilians*, pardon their
French, for a stunt like this one. I'm already
uncomfortable in my borrowed flight suit, which

is cut for someone a lot taller and skinnier than yours truly, and the chute harness digs into me in several intimate ways at once, and being lectured by Major Icy Cool about how to make the oxygen mask mike work while sliding down a guideline from one plane to another at thirty-eight thousand feet and 440 miles an hour is real hard to concentrate on.

I have to do this, I think, past it all, *I have to, it has to be me, I'm the one who's being haunted, no one else can do it, fuck my life*, and it is a comfort to see Captain Warner flickering into and out of existence behind Major Cool, even if it makes it even harder to concentrate on what he's telling me: seeing Warner means *I got it right*, that I *am* supposed to be here, that I haven't fucked up catastrophically—yet—and that this whole song-and-dance has some small chance of actually working. That I finally get what he was trying to tell me all along.

He's your best hope, I think, and God I hope the plane was right.

We're coming up on the BrightAir 737. Based on the pattern it's demonstrated so far, it pops into existence for about a hundred ninety minutes at a time, continuing on its flightpath without deviation, and then vanishes for anywhere up to six hours before reappearing. Just to be extra annoying, it doesn't seem to reappear where one might expect it *along* that flightpath given how fast it's going when it's present; we can't predict exactly where it's going to show up, just that it will be back *somewhere* along that path at some point in the near future. Round and round the world it goes, the most ridiculous satellite of all time, serenely undisturbed by how much of a giant fucking pain in the ass it's being to worldwide aviation.

Because it's orbiting the planet way slower than the Earth is turning—it's only doing 440 mph to the Earth's 1000-some—the ground track of the plane's path along its vector is basically describing a series of sine-wave patterns across the map that the people at NASA have been tracking for us with the same software they use to track normal *helpful* satellites. The one good thing about this situation is that based on that tracking it doesn't seem to be changing altitude at all, so ATC around the world can just block out its flight level and heading, clearing that altitude and airspace of any other directed traffic, and drop the danger of collision a long way down—not *gone*, but decreased significantly, which is a relief.

The news stations had done their best to downplay the situation, but there'd been zero chance for a cover-up: people knew there was a rogue plane in the sky, that it wasn't a military exercise, and that as of right now nobody was sure what the fuck to do about it—which went over just about as well as you'd imagine. Hasty working groups had been convened between various governmental entities to discuss options; as concept after concept ran into the simple fact that *the plane could not do what it was, in fact, doing* in a sane and sensible world, less sane and less sensible ideas began to seem more inviting.

It had disappeared two hours ago this time, and ACARS had reacquired it forty minutes back, upon which me and Dooley were rushed on board *this* hideous plane and roared up into the sky to intercept. The whole business has been kind of like a cross between a relay race and a kind of weird aerial dance that reminds me a bit of the counterintuitive calculus of orbital mechanics: launching a ship at an angle and velocity to rendezvous with where some celestial body *would be* in several days' time. We knew where it was *likely* to be—not so far from where it had disappeared, over eastern Nebraska—and sort of when-ish it might possibly be there, but this part was basically a question of transporting us to the nearest air base to wherever the thing was probably going to pop back into existence, which happened to be Offutt AFB, in time for us to go catch it as soon as it arrived. Not one of the military's more crisply efficient operations, but there isn't exactly a useful precedent for this kind of shit.

"You're gonna have one shot at this!" Major Cool yells over the rattle and clank of the

Stratotanker. "There's thirty minutes of air in those bottles, so once you get on board, either turn the pressure on or get down below ten thousand feet in a hurry unless you want to pass out. You miss on that first shot, we haul you back and plan to try again next time the thing shows up, understand?"

I flash him a thumbs-up and privately vow that they are absolutely not going to have to winch my tubby ass back into their horrible plane for another attempt: I have had it with this entire situation and I am not sure I will have the guts to *try* a second time. What I can see of Dooley's face behind the mask and helmet visor is a very gross unhealthy color and I have just about enough spare brain to wonder if he's as close to puking as I am, and if he's gonna do so at a super inopportune moment, and then I simply cannot think about Doolarino anymore because Major Cool's pal has pulled a lever and a huge part of the back of the goddamn plane cracks open to let in brilliant vicious light and a howling frozen wind—and there it is.

It looks so *ordinary*. The blue-white-teal BrightAir livery, the familiar shape of the thing, trundling along its diurnal course exactly as if it is not some kind of fucking weird revenant from another dimension where planes don't need gas to fly; it sends cold daggers through my guts, a misery that has nothing to do with motion. We're ahead of it, about twenty feet above, flying in perfect formation with the thing. I can see very clearly where Major Cool's magnetic grapple is supposed to land and lodge, above the forward door in the fuselage, and I can also see the lever that unlocks and opens that door—which we'll only be able to open with considerable difficulty given the slipstream but which we *can* open because the cabin's depressurized—and then Dooley beside me turns to thump me on the helmet, give me a thumbs-up, and I give him one back, and our lines are clipped to the cable and Major Cool is ready to take aim and suddenly everything is happening too fast.

It almost works. Almost. I resent how close it comes to working, if you get what I mean: clear and present evidence of the universe having a goddamn laugh at our expense. Major Cool, behind his aviators, aims and fires his magnetic grapple; we can't hear the clang of metal on metal over the roaring of the wind, but it's visibly stuck to the side of the BrightAir plane, and first Dooley's and then my harness are clipped to the line, and I just about have time to wonder if I'm going to be able to jump out of the goddamn aircraft before Major Cool's colleague gives us both a healthy shove between the shoulderblades and suddenly everything is very bright and very loud and freezing fucking cold even through the insulation of the flightsuit. There's no time to be terrified: I'm flung sideways, the harness digging into me with the force of it, and then we are right there, plastered against the outside of a ghost plane from another dimension, and Dooley is grabbing the lever on the outside of the door, white and rivet-pimpled and too ordinary for words—the stenciled letters, CAUTION ESCAPE SLIDE IS ARMED in red beneath the handle, are exactly like I've seen them a thousand times on the ground, and he shoves the handle hard and the door shudders and swings inward like it's supposed to. We know to expect the bright-yellow escape slide since the flight attendants would have armed it prior to takeoff, and there is a non-zero chance that it could get stuck in one of the engines or damage the tail as it tears away from the plane, but it extends and releases without incident and flashes past and is gone, and right up until Dooley loses his grip I think everything is going to be just fine.

There are cases in the literature of people being sucked out of planes at altitude and cracking their heads open like an eggshell against the fuselage with the force of the 400-mile-an-hour wind rushing past. Dooley doesn't hit his head on the edge of the doorframe, which is a small mercy; it's his right forearm that goes *snap* like a branch breaking under a bitter weight of winter ice, a sound I can hear with weird clarity even over the roar of the wind.

He somehow manages not to scream, and even more impressively manages to hold his shit together long enough to get *inside* the plane and unclip his harness from the line that's still holding us tethered to the Stratotanker flying twenty feet overhead, and I follow him in, tumbling headfirst onto the kind of ugly utilitarian carpet you see in every passenger airliner flying. As soon as the watchers in the other plane see that I'm unclipped from the cable the Stratotanker draws away, pulling the magnetic grapple free of the 737's fuselage, and peels off to the left, banking sharply away from us. God knows how I manage to wrestle the door back into position and latch it shut, but a moment later Dooley and I are staring at one another inside an upsettingly ordinary passenger plane, the silence deafening after the howling wind outside.

I am weirdly hyper-aware of the way in which he takes up space, the realness and solidity of him, the only other fragment of the normal world in a plane that has become entirely and completely *abnormal*—and he looks like complete hell. Behind the mask his face is grey. He's breathing sharply through clenched teeth, his right arm cradled against his chest; the arm is ever so slightly bending at an angle that arms are not meant to bend at, which makes me feel kind of sick to observe. There is absolutely nothing left of the slick hyper-competent obnoxious asshole he normally portrays, and *man* do I miss that guy, because the alternative is *I'm* the one in charge.

As far as I can see, we're alone in the plane: there's no one in any of the rows of seats clearly visible. All the oxygen masks have dropped, yellow cups and plastic bags hanging down in a dangling forest of tubing that makes me think weirdly of seaweed, but there's nobody trying to suck air from them, just as there had been no one sitting in the cockpit when I'd pushed myself through, all the way back in DC, staring into my crystal. No evidence that anyone had ever *been* there, either. No pocket change, no watches, no false teeth, no pacemakers or fake joints or titanium bone screws, any more than there had been up front in the cockpit. All one hundred forty-whatever people who'd taken off from Reagan National and whatever they'd been wearing are presumably stacked and holding somewhere *else*, awaiting clearance that's not going to be granted. Same thing's going to happen to us unless we move with some alacrity.

I wonder absurdly if their luggage is still down below in the cargo hold, or if that also got left behind in whatever dimension this thing keeps blinking into. Of course, it might not be the plane itself that's doing the blinking; it could be something *else* behind the pattern of

disappearances. I think of the thing that killed
Warner's plane, the thing inside that impossible
storm that looked up at me and *smiled* in
Warner's witchwalking dream, and—

—what if it wasn't the only one? What if
something *like that* has been delicately taking
this aircraft in and out of the world, tasting it
each time? I think of the freak storm the jet pilots
mentioned, when the plane disappeared for the
first time, and wonder what was inside it, and
whether it smiled the same way.

Christ but I wish I hadn't just thought of that.

The 737 seems reasonably solid underneath
us, at least, even if by the clock on the instrument
panel we only have about forty minutes left
before it's scheduled to vanish—if it follows the
pattern, now that we've changed the game by
finding our way on board, *please* let it follow
the pattern—and only *thirty* minutes worth
of breathable air unless we can get the cabin
press back again. We need to get down *now*,
and Doolarino needs someone to make his arm
not have an extra bend in it, also *now*. He's still
sweating like it's ninety degrees in here, his hair
dark at the temples with it. I've broken a bone
or two in my time and that kind of pain is not
conducive to clear thought patterns; I won't be
able to count on the guy to help me out much
at all, and the goddamn pointless *stupidity* of
letting him come all the way up here in the first

place is clearer than ever. It wasn't like I had a hell of a lot of choice: when Dooley sets his mind to something he's as stubborn as bedrock, but still, if I'm wrong about all this, it's going to be such a fucking *waste* of that irreplaceable brain.

This isn't helping; I'm wasting minutes we don't have being sorry for what I can't change. Time to see if Captain Warner finally, finally wants to make himself useful, instead of bleeding meaningfully at me while I try to do my job.

I haul myself to my feet by hanging on to an aisle seat and offer Dooley a hand up. After a moment he takes it, and his fingers are ice-cold with shock. "You gonna be okay?" I ask, knowing full well how stupid of a question it is, and he glares at me, which weirdly makes me feel a little better: we're back on familiar ground.

"I'm just fine," he grits out, muffled behind his oxygen mask, but at least he's on his feet, and he follows me into the cockpit. The door's open, which saves us the trouble of breaking it down with whatever's available at hand, and I wonder why; since 9/11 the cockpit's been sacrosanct, no one but the flight crew allowed access. That it's open is weird, but it's also pretty much the first thing that's gone right since we started this whole dumbass operation, and it's the first thing that makes me feel like something might actually be on our side. It's a strange flicker of—serenity, I guess, a brief sensation of calm inside all the terror, like

I'd felt sitting on the 747's wing and listening to it lecture me on flight control surfaces.

I unfasten the straps of my chute harness and climb out of it—that's a relief, that thing had been digging into me in a thoroughly importunate way—and set the chute down. Can't fit into the pilot's seat with that strapped to my back, and if we need to bail out I'd hopefully have enough time to put the thing back on before jumping, if I was able to make myself jump at all.

The cockpit's exactly the way it was in my vision, exactly the way a 737 always looks. Sunlight pours across the instruments, dust motes bright in the air. The control yokes move ever so slightly as the autopilot keeps us flying perfectly on course. It's so fucking *normal*, except for those CABIN ALTITUDE and TAKEOFF CONFIG warning lights on the overhead panel.

Dooley is leaning behind me in the open doorway, his arm cradled against his chest. "Well?" he demands, sounding a bit more like the Dooley I know. "I thought you had a fucking plan, Stacy. Tell me you have a plan other than staring at the goddamn controls like an idiot."

"I do," I say, feeling that weird touch of *serenity* again, and just like that we're not alone in the cockpit: Warner is here too, standing behind the captain's seat, spectral and gruesome as usual. I look at him, raising my eyebrows, and he nods his half of a head at the seat in front of him, so after another moment I climb into it myself, very much aware of all the controls *right there*, at my fingertips, underneath my feet. "Take the other side," I tell Dooley. "You have to talk to the ground for me. I can't do that and try to fly this thing."

"*You* can't fly this thing at all," says Dooley, but he takes off his chute harness and settles into the right-hand seat. "You have to get fucking *possessed* by your ghost pilot guy in order to fly it, so make with the spirit-possession, and I can't believe I just said that."

"Look up at the panel over your head," I tell him. I shouldn't need to tell him, but shock makes you slow. "See the cabin press knob?"

He does, and I can tell he's thinking how weird it is to see one of these things in its original context, rather than in the smoking wreckage of a dead plane. "Yeah," he says, sounding a little better.

"Set it to auto," I say, and a moment later, there's a hiss and my ears begin to hurt as the 737's systems begin to bring the cabin altitude down to where it ought to be. That's the second thing that's gone right: the unlocked cockpit door, and the fact that bleed air from the plane's jet engines is being supplied to the air-conditioning packs that run the cabin pressurization system: we *can* make this thing do what we want it to. So far.

Quite soon now you will need to pay attention, the 747 in my dream had said.

I reach for the seatbelt straps and pull them over my shoulders, and as the buckle clicks shut I have just enough time to understand what's about to happen to me before Warner is not standing behind the seat at all, Warner is *in* the seat because Warner is *in me*, almost the way Desi had been *in me* but far less politely. There is a long, miserable moment of swimming dizziness that threatens to make me puke all over the goddamn controls, and then I stop trying to be in charge of my own body and—pull back, and float. It feels a little bit like it must feel to take the first breath of water as you're drowning: the instinct is to fight it as long as you can, knowing failure is inevitable, but after that first breath, everything gets simpler in a hurry.

Warner is in me, in my head, feeling his way through my neural pathways, testing his control over my body, the way you adjust the mirrors and move the seat when you get into a rental car. Beside us, Dooley is staring, white visible all the way around his grey irises, and I wonder what it actually looks like from the outside; if there's clear visible tells that I'm no longer driving. It's *weird*, having someone else in charge of stuff like breathing—I'd been afraid of that, the moment when a dead dude would have to remember how the whole autonomic nervous system thing worked, but after a moment of brief confusion he seems to have got it straightened out. He breathes

differently than I do. More deeply. He's used to
a larger set of ribs.

The TAKEOFF CONFIG warning light had
gone out when Dooley set the press selector to
auto; now the CABIN ALTITUDE light goes
out as well, the indicated altitude reading eight
thousand feet again, just where it should be.
Warner reaches up with my hands and releases
the oxygen mask's catches, takes off our helmet
… and after a moment Dooley does the same,
awkwardly one-handed. Neither of us appears any
the worse for breathing the cockpit atmosphere,
which is encouraging. It smells like planes always
do: plastic and faintly like kerosene and cleaning
products, mixed with whatever that day's lunch
entrée had been.

"Mr. Dooley," says Warner, and hilariously
our voice cracks; he's used to a slightly different
larynx as well, and it takes a few tries for him to
use mine without sounding like a teenage boy
in the most embarrassing stage of puberty. "Put
on your headset and tune the radio to 121.5."
He puts on our own headset, adjusts the mike,
and despite everything I feel an undeniable little
frisson of pleasure at *telling Dooley what to do*.
Warner closes our hands around the control yoke,
and I can feel an echo of his own satisfaction
at having both hands to fly with; his thumb
flicks the stabilizer trim switch on one side of
the yoke and Dooley flinches as the black trim

wheels either side of the pedestal start to turn, the plane's stabilizers adjusting themselves to Warner's command, fine-tuning the way it is pushing through the air.

Dooley's been watching all of this in a worrying kind of blank horror, but he's managed to twist the radio knob to the emergency frequency nonetheless; once that's done Warner thumbs the push-to-talk switch on the yoke, and says the words you never want to hear on the air, no matter what, still so weird in my distorted voice: "Mayday Mayday Mayday. This is BrightAir 291 declaring an emergency. We are at flight level 380, heading 335, airspeed 440, northwest of Omaha, requesting vectors for nearest available airport."

There's a stunned pause, and then the radio crackles and spits out "BrightAir 291, Minneapolis Center, understand emergency, can you advise fuel and souls on board?"

At this point Dooley, who has been staring white-faced at the radio, jumps in. "Minneapolis, we have to get this thing on the ground before it *vanishes underneath of us,* time's kind of crucial here—"

Another voice comes on the air. "Minneapolis Center, this is Offutt control, divert all incoming traffic away from Eppley Field until further notice. We'll take over from here. BrightAir two niner one, we have you on radar, turn left heading 124 and contact Offutt tower on 123.7."

Warner reaches out, twiddles a couple of knobs on the control panel, and turns the yoke to the left; the plane begins to bank in a long sweeping turn. I don't even want to think about the pain in the ass this is shaping up to be for the poor fuckers charged with routing Nebraska air traffic, and luckily I don't have a lot of spare brains to devote to their plight. The Air Force is basically taking ownership of the situation, which is probably the best option available.

Dooley switches frequencies. "Uh, Offutt tower, this is BrightAir 291," he says. He's still grey and sweating and I don't want to look at his right arm, but he sounds a little more like himself, i.e. obnoxious. "You want to tell us what to do next?"

"Who am I speaking to?" asks the tower.

"Chief Investigator Dooley, NTSB," says Dooley. "I got, uh ... as far as I know, either one or two other souls on board. And apparently lots of fuel."

The tower is silent for a fraction of a moment. "Understood, total of three individuals." You can hear the incredulity in the clipped radio voice; it's easy to picture the controllers staring at one another wondering what the hell happened to the rest of the people on board. Me too, guy, I think. Me fucking too. "BrightAir, you are cleared for an emergency descent, maintain heading 123, we're vectoring you in for runway 12."

"BrightAir 291, beginning emergency descent," says Warner, who has now become used to my vocal cords and doesn't sound quite so risible, and pushes the control column forward, deploys the speed brakes. Dooley curses under his breath as he is tilted forward against his straps, bumping his bad arm, and I have time to wonder if he's gonna nick some blood vessel on a sharp edge of bone with all this moving around, and if there's a single goddamn thing I can do about it. Beneath us the green flatness of Nebraska is getting noticeably closer.

"You said it wasn't the langoliers," Dooley says, sounding a bit better, a bit less spacy, possibly because of the pain. "You have any idea what it *is*? Are we gonna be allowed to put this thing on the ground, or will it just wink out with us on board before we get there?"

"We'll find out," says Warner, paying attention to the plane rather than Dooley, which Dools does not like in the slightest.

"Jesus *Christ*, that's fucking creepy," he says. "I want to talk to Stacy, okay? Tell me Stacy's still in there." He actually sounds concerned, and I briefly wonder what the hell he'd do if Warner told him *no*.

"Yes," says Warner without so much as a pause or glance at Dools. "Offutt tower, BrightAir 291, say distance to threshold."

The tower gives him a number, and I can

feel my face going grim without knowing why. "What?" says Dooley, staring at us. "What is it?"

"We're too high," says Warner. "I can't get us down in that distance at this descent rate, and we don't have a lot of time left." He's looking at the clock readout, and I realize more time has passed than I had been aware of, in the process of getting on board and contacting the ground; if the plane keeps to the pattern we've seen over the past day and a half it's going to vanish underneath of us in about twenty-three minutes, give or take. We're still at twenty thousand feet. I don't know what the 737's maximum sink rate is, but based on the way Warner feels in my head, it's not good.

"There's the airport," Dooley says, very pale. "Airfield. Whatever." He points; in the distance I can see the elongated trapezoid Popsicle-shape of a runway far below us, approaching fast but still much too small.

"Offutt tower," says Warner. "BrightAir 291. I'm going to have to slip it."

"Say again?" the radio asks, and before I can even begin to prepare myself he drops the nose, applies left rudder, and twists the control yoke hard the opposite way—and the 737 *slews* downward, descending at a sharper angle, losing altitude in a hurry.

I know what he is doing not so much because he's in my head—I can't really hear what he is thinking—but because I've seen this maneuver before, read about it in an emergency landing back in the eighties. I can only hope to fuck that Warner is as good at his job as the pilot of that jet had been.

Dooley is cursing in a raw hoarse monotone, clutching his hurt arm to his chest, and warning lights and horns are going off like a goddamn Christmas tree as Warner flings us at the ground, straining my muscles in the effort to hold the forward slip steady. The plane is rattling and groaning all around us as its airframe is pushed to the limits, and I'm only slightly glad I don't know what those are.

I have no idea how long it is before he straightens out, but the ground is a *lot* closer, and he calls out to Dooley, wanting flaps and slats—and Dooley freezes.

He knows how the fucking flaps work, there's a lever sticking up from the pedestal that says FLAPS on it in big old capital letters, he's seen it a million times, but Dooley's blood has got to be about half and half adrenaline and fatigue poisons at this point, and he simply stares at us, grey-white and sweating. He's so pale that the grey of his eyes looks almost violet, blank and shocked, his lips bloodless. I can *feel* Warner making the decision a second before he deliberately pulls back just enough to let *me* reach for the control with the hand we share, and a second later I'm dizzy all over again because I'm not hearing his own voice in my mouth, I'm hearing a different voice in my *head*: the plane, from the dream. *Flaps*, it says, matter-of-fact. *Like I showed you*.

Warner's still got hold of the yoke with our other hand, but for some reason he's letting *me* close my fingers around the lever and pull it down, clicking through each detent all the way to 40—and god, I can *feel* the way the plane responds, the difference in lift, it's kind of amazing, just like it had been when the 747 showed me how the fucking things worked—Christ, had I really heard that just now, was it somehow *here with us*, watching this whole nightmare go down?

Remember about cockpit resource management, by the way, it had said before. *Too many of them don't*.

Whatever had made Warner give me control, just for that moment, has passed; he's firmly back in charge of our body, and I think again of the 747's voice: *He'll help. He's actually your best hope, although you won't realize that for a while yet*.

It hadn't been wrong. In that stretched-out nightmare time I reach for it, blindly, wanting any shred of confidence, of courage. *Who are you? What's happening?*

I told you not to ask stupid questions, says the voice, and it is no longer just the voice of my dream-747 but of something vast, something impossible to perceive, echoing in the hollow places of my skull. *When you get this far out into cosmological shit, to borrow a phrase, you got to throw away the instruction manual. Now land this plane, and take these people home.*

What people? but I think unbidden of the thing that had looked up at me at Mount Storm, before Warner died the first time, and wonder again if it is somehow related to the thing that has been tasting this plane as it slips between realities, and know with the sudden certitude of a shatterbomb that the voice of the 747 is *not that thing*: it is something else, a balance, a force of its own. Something that wants us to *live*—

—and the runway is much nearer, the runway looks like it's actually possible to touch now, rather than a distant thought smudged on the ground—Warner calls for landing gear, and this time Dooley has enough presence of mind to grab the lever and pull it down; we all look as the telltales light up one by one: down and three green, locked, thank *fuck* for that—

—and the radio is yelling at us and Warner is not answering, Warner is *floating* the huge plane down the last fifty feet, flares gently, raising the nose for a moment, engines idle, and then the main gear touch down with only the hint of a bounce, the nose comes down, the runway markings strobing ahead of us as we roar down the concrete—he closes our hand on the thrust reverser levers, pulls them all the way up, and inertia presses us forward against the straps for the few seconds the reversers are deployed—slowing now, slowing, the lines on the runway turning into individual strokes rather than a flashing streak.

We're down. With—thirteen minutes to go.

Warner rolls us to wheelstop, and there's a moment of blessed, terrifying silence before the sirens of the emergency crash tenders approach from all directions. I can feel it when he withdraws his influence, letting me have control of my body once again. Both Dooley and I are panting, our hearts still hammering with spent adrenaline, and when the sounds begin from behind us I think we both scream a little, used to the silence of the vacant plane.

Because it isn't empty anymore. They're back. The dead, empty silence is gone.

Beyond the closed cockpit door it sounds like the cabin is *full* of people, talking, laughing, bitching, shouting, demanding to know why the oxygen masks are down and why there are all these fire trucks around the plane: *living people,* somehow back from wherever the fuck they'd gone, sounding like they'd missed the entire fucking drama. Dooley and I stare at one another, frozen, and it is Warner who takes control again for one last time. He reaches out my hand for the intercom and says with my voice, "Cabin crew, evacuate the aircraft. Evacuate, evacuate, evacuate."

It's like a spell: you have to say the word

three times before it works, but it *does* work; we can hear the flight attendants swing into action, hear the hiss-*thwup* sound as the doors open and the long yellow tongue of one evacuation slide extends on the right side of the plane from the door Dooley and I didn't open; the other slide must have come to earth somewhere in the Dissected Till Plains. The slide bounces and jerks as people start tumbling down it. People who *were not there* twenty minutes ago, up in the empty reaches of the sky.

All of this seems impossible, but it is still happening anyway, and Dooley is shaking me with his good hand and saying something I can't hear over the noise from the cabin. Someone is trying to get into the cockpit, the doorknob twisting back and forth, and that's finally enough to jolt me out of the daze. It is *hard* to unbuckle the straps and push myself to my feet: my knees have no strength at all, little sacks of water— and it's only after I steady myself, holding on to the back of the captain's seat, that I realize I'm alone in my body once again, and that I'm holding Chief Investigator Wayne Dooley's good hand tight enough that our knuckles are white. I think it's possibly the fourth time in my life that I've *touched* Dooley, and he's hanging on to me panicky-tight with an expression I've never seen on that particular patrician face, and for a brief and impossibly strange moment, I wonder what it would be like to kiss him.

(I don't kiss people. Not much, anyway, and the idea of kissing *this* particular person is, no, what the fuck, but just for a second, just then, with all the sharp familiar architecture of Dooley's face for once not set in any of his ordinary fuck-you-I'm-in-control expressions, just then, I wonder what it'd be like.)

And then reality comes back all at once. Dooley's managed to get himself unbuckled one-handed. Warner's still behind the controls, and I cannot spare the time to say anything to him because I want to get me and Dooley off this fucking thing before it decides to vanish back to the twilight zone. I unlock the cabin door and stand aside as two men in pilot's uniforms rush in, yelling, and stop short at the sight of Warner still in the captain's seat.

Shock-pale, the chief flight attendant stares at us. "What's happening? Who are you? Who is *that?*"

Because there is Warner, *whole and visible*, sitting in the left-hand seat and shutting down the plane's systems one by one. He's solid. Somehow he is solid, just for long enough.

"Long story," I tell her. "Emergency landing. We have to get off this plane *right now*, this guy's hurt." I give Dooley a little shove in her direction and her training kicks back in. She sends Dooley down the slide first and follows him; I'm next, stumbling out into light and warmth and air that isn't moving four hundred miles an hour and then, finally, I'm *on solid ground*.

You're supposed to fold your arms and jump out onto the slide with your legs stretched out like you're doing a Cossack dance, land on your ass and slither to safety, but of course what I do is end up rolling down it like a fucking clown and nearly snapping my neck, and I'm so dizzy I can hardly stand when I get to the bottom. There are hands, rough but kind hands in heavy gloves, helping me up, asking if I'm hurt, and I keep telling them *no, it's Dooley, he broke his goddamn arm, he's in shock, go fix him instead*, and we are all being shepherded away from the plane which the fire guys are eyeing suspiciously in case it decides to suddenly burst into flame. I look back, over my shoulder, and although the two pilots have followed us down the slide to safety, I can see Captain Warner in the cockpit window very clearly and know he can see me.

Because he has his eyes, this time. He's not the bloody revenant that's been hanging around ever since the Mount Storm crash.

As I watch, he sketches me a little salute.

I nod and let the paramedics draw me away, let them help me into an ambulance, despite the fact I'm not the one who's hurt—and when the shouting behind me begins I do not need to turn around again to know that the plane has vanished, slide and all.

It's gone for good, this time. I *know* it's gone, and so is he, I know it as well as I know my own name. As somebody wraps a space blanket around my shoulders and puts a cup of terrible too-sweet coffee into my hands they are asking what happened, and I almost laugh but manage not to because when you start laughing like that you *do not stop* until somebody hits you, and my head hurts enough already. In the back of my mind I hear the 747 again, or the voice of whatever had been behind it all along: *when you get into cosmological shit like this, you got to throw away the instruction manual.*

"A pilot landed the plane, is what happened," I say. "Not the guys who took off, but it was a pilot who got us down again." I don't add *ask me how I know,* and in the next ambulance over, Dooley—wrapped in a space-blanket of his own, his wrecked arm hastily splinted—yells, with the unerring instinct of the lifelong civil servant, **"No further comment!"**

I can't help laughing then, a little, despite it all. The absurdity of the situation is impossible to ignore, as is the euphoria of *being on the ground* again, safe on Mother Earth and not miles up in the sky in a crate piloted by a dead man or a vanished man or something worse than either: the ground is going nowhere, it is not going to vanish underneath me, and if I never ever have to go up in another aircraft for the rest of my natural fucking life I am okay with that. Rail travel is a thing. We still have the automobile. Hell, I'll even try a transatlantic cruise rather than go up there again. The point is that *it's no longer my responsibility*; the point is that everything, right now, is someone else's problem than my own. It's an exhilarating feeling.

I don't know what to make of that one brief, weird moment in the cockpit right after we landed, when Dooley's good hand had found mine and clutched it almost hard enough to hurt. I think it's just something that happens when you've just *nearly* died: an instinctive desire to cling to whoever's been through hell with you, to prove you're both still breathing. That it's over, and you made it through, and even if almost no one else in the whole wide world will ever really understand what you'll never be able to forget, hey, at least there's one other person who does. That you aren't entirely alone in that impossible memory. That you're still you, on the other side.

As they close the ambulance doors I am aware of never having been so tired in *ever*—but it's a good kind of tired, I think. A weird job well done.

Story of my life.

*

You'd be surprised how quickly people forget

things they don't want to remember. Or that they can't make sense out of; it's a human self-defense mechanism against the great howling wild inchoate universe and the myriad creative ways in which it tries to drive you mad.

Either they forget it, or they get a six-figure book deal and never shut up about it *ever again*. The split was basically fifty-fifty for the BrightAir passengers and crew (the pilots, I heard, both took early retirement and refused to talk about it or set foot on a plane again, and I don't blame 'em, even if I ended up breaking my own never-flying-again rule). Pilots aside, for months afterward the talk shows were packed with excited interviews about titles like DARK LANDING and FLIGHT 291: MY JOURNEY INTO TERROR and ON BOARD THE GHOST PLANE, not all of which were ghostwritten (more's the pity). They all told essentially the same story, with varying levels of sophistication: from the point of view of the people on board, the entire episode had lasted only half an hour or so, beginning with them passing out or falling asleep or being put under a sinister spell of some description, followed by awakening as the wheels touched down at Offutt and finding the forest of oxygen masks dropped and apparently some kind of emergency crew at the controls. Even the most devoted ghostwriter could make only so much of that sequence of events, and it faded from the talk circuits after about six months, ending up parodied on *SNL* at least once. I watched it with a sixpack next to me, and only winced a couple of times.

The NatGeo people showed up at the NTSB wanting to start talks about featuring BrightAir 291 on their air-crash-investigation show, but since it wasn't actually a crash and the Board had absolutely no clue what had caused the incident, the discussion didn't go far. It was marked off as simply *an incident*, and the company paid a stupid amount of money to the families in order to avoid a lengthy and complex trial, and the Board's official investigation eventually wrapped up with a finding of *unspecified*. Since there was no plane to be examined, *unspecified* was the best they could do.

That's one way to put it.

BrightAir changed its name shortly after the settlement, the way ValuJet had to back in the 90s, but nobody was fooled; after another couple of months it was announced that Southwest was acquiring what was left of it, and I heard where some of the ex-BrightAir planes had been exorcised before anybody would consent to fly them, as if whatever had happened to 291 had contaminated the rest of the fleet—and who's to say it didn't? Sloshing some holy water around and bell-book-and-candling couldn't hurt, after all.

We're still looking for a physical cause for the

Helios syndrome. So far we haven't got anywhere, but maybe bringing together new branches of investigation might yield some clues. I say *we*, as in *Contingency Communications Specialist Serensky and I*. Desi hadn't thought much of my government job, but when I got back from this particular little jaunt and told her what I'd been fucking around with—weird-ass magic, shit moving between worlds, ghost pilots, mysterious talking dream-planes, danger and excitement *and* government benefits? Compared to earning $25 an hour providing ad hoc therapy to the living on behalf of the dead (and selling batik caftans), suddenly working for The Man didn't seem so bad. She'd gotten herself a change of attitude and a cute Agent Scully pantsuit and knocked on Dooley's door, and somehow the staffing budget had miraculously stretched to two plausibly-deniable consultant positions rather than just one.

She's come up with some ways to test pieces of airplane wreckage for the residue of hostile magic, kinda the way you look for explosive residue on bits of the fuselage after a crash. Together we're going through all the recovered FedEx fragments to work out if they fell foul of some kind of sorcery. Dooley and his goons are down the hall in the main lab, and sometimes one of them will come watch us do our thing and ask questions, and sometimes the questions are even smart ones.

(I don't know what it was that grabbed hold of BrightAir 291 and played with it, slipped it in and out of reality. I don't know if it was the same thing I saw in that unnatural storm that killed Captain Warner's plane, the thing that saw *me*. I also don't know what spoke to me in the voice of my imaginary 747 and told me what to do—I may never know—but I *do* know they're different: the one is hungry, wanting, *devouring*, and the other is ... patient. Vast, and patient, and kind *because* it's patient. Maybe one day Desi and I can figure out what the hell to call the two of them, but somehow I doubt it, if you know what I mean.)

Me, I think what killed the FedEx plane is pretty much on the supernatural end of the spectrum in terms of likely causality, but Dooley maintains it's a physical fault they just haven't tracked down yet. He's got visions of a latter-day 737-rudder-hardover type revelation that will cement his name into the ranks of top-achieving NTSB investigators. Hey, who knows: a stopped clock is right twice a day, after all.

I haven't seen Warner since that moment on the tarmac, just before the BrightAir plane disappeared, and I'm pretty sure I'm never going to see him again. In a weird way, I'm kinda going to miss that guy, gross as his spectral manifestation might have been, but I'm okay with it. I think he is too, wherever he is now. I know how much we owe him, not just Dooley and I and the other people on the plane he landed, but everyone else around the world who was affected by that impossible, terrifying flight, even if they'll never know his name.

Dooley's arm isn't exactly as good as new; it's got a bunch of titanium in it that sets off the TSA scanners. He says it hurts when the weather changes, but he can still write reams and reams of his terrible chicken-scratch handwriting in his terrible, yellow legal pads, so I guess that's okay. He can also mix a pretty decent dirty martini, which I found out about a month after the landing. Out of the blue he called me up and asked if I'd been having freaktastic dreams about being back on the plane or if that was special to just him, and did I want to discuss this further at his penthouse condo overlooking the Potomac. Turns out there isn't a squadron of groupies or a 50s housewife waiting for him at home, but there is one hell of a view.

I still don't know what it's like to kiss Chief Investigator Wayne Dooley, but it seems like I might get to find out, one of these days. This is a conflict of interest, of course, but hey, the federal government claims I don't officially exist. What they don't know probably won't hurt them.

One thing hasn't changed, though, and that's the fact that I'm apparently stuck with weird-as-fuck dreams starring the talking 747. I don't mind, actually. It gives me an advantage.

My flying instructor keeps saying she doesn't get how I know half the shit I come up with, and I keep telling her a guy has to keep *some* secrets, doesn't he?